D0744664

Woodston

A Sequel to Jane Austen's 'Northanger Abbey'

Kate Westwood

Published by Kate Westwood
www.katewestwood.net

ISBN: 978-0-6450494-2-8

Illustrations by Anung Prihantoko

Disclaimer

This is a work of fiction. Names, characters, places,
organisations, events, and incidents are either products of the
author's imagination or used fictitiously.

Books by Kate Westwood

A Scandal at Delford

Beauty and the Beast of Thornleigh

A Bath Affair

The Value of an Anne Elliot

Woodston

KATE WESTWOOD

Acknowledgements

Acknowledgements: I would like to thank Anung Prihantoko for the beautiful illustrations, Dreamstone Publishing for formatting and other help, and Cathy Walker for her wonderful cover design as usual.

Table of Contents

'Upon this conviction, she would not be surprized if even in Henry [...] one slight imperfection might hereafter appear'

–Jane Austen, *Northanger Abbey*

One

Early October, 1798

Catherine Moreland, without claim to any particularly remarkable antecedents, herself being the recipient of an adequate but undistinguished education, and boasting tolerably pretty but not exceptional looks, felt herself the most fortunate girl in the whole of England. As she stepped from the carriage and took her new husband's offered arm, she wondered if anyone had ever been so happy as she was at that moment.

Natural modesty had allowed her to concede that she could not, as her mother and father had pointed out numerous times in the last year, do any better considering her own unremarkable station in life. Her father was a clergyman and had the parsonage at Fullerton, Catherine's home. While not exactly poor, Mr Moreland had neither the means nor the consequence to provide his oldest daughter with a large income or that rank which would bring wealthy beaux to her doorstep. He could provide her with merely four hundred pounds a year, and that, for a young lady of modest origins, must be fortune enough. She had been brought up to be humble, and never in expectation of more than she deserved. But in catching the eye of a tolerably set-up young man such as Henry Tilney, the youngest son of General Tilney of Northanger and heir to a comfortable stipend sometime in the future, Catherine had managed to elevate herself to a station neither she nor her parents had expected.

Expected or not, however, this new situation in life she was willing to embrace with all the natural eagerness and optimism which love could furnish her with. Now, as she stood on the semi-circled sweep of a gravelled driveway, eyeing the pretty stone house which was to be her home, love, or whatever it was which passed for love with young and inexperienced females of eighteen years, would allow her to admit no fault with the vision before her. Woodston parsonage was not only handsome and agreeable, it was utterly charming, simply because it was Henry's home and therefore her own.

Although it was not the oldest building in the area, the large, white-stoned house formed the central focus of the bustling village of Woodston, being at the end of the village and thus commanding the view from almost every street as the eye was led to its pleasing, distant form. It was tolerably disengaged from the rest of the village which gave it an air of distinction, without its being at all superior. It had been built only thirty years ago, having succeeded a much older and rougher building which Henry's father, General Tilney, had insisted be torn down, despite its history. And despite the building's comparative newness, the parsonage had been already refurbished ten years ago at the General's insistence, for the General had a passionate regard for modernisation, whether that be in his gardens, his furnishings, his carriages or in the buildings which populated his estate.

To a new-married woman, entering her own home for the first time, nothing could appear more auspicious than the pretty picture made by the elegant stone house before Catherine. To be sure, Woodston was not as grand as Northanger, nor did it command the solemn respect which the other house did; Northanger Abbey boasted as much ancient history and gothic appearance as Woodston did not. But her new home was larger and much prettier than the old parsonage Catherine had grown up in and left behind her. It boasted no small number of rooms, its large windows were plenty in number, its outlook pleasant from most sides of the house, and it was surrounded by some exceedingly pretty parklands. Due to the season, these were now fully decked in a splendour of golds and reds and made as pretty a picture as Catherine had ever graced to witness. Woodston, she thought complacently, was a most charming home, and she and Henry the most charming and fortunate couple in the world!

"*Woodston parsonage was not only handsome and agreeable, it was utterly charming.*"

She turned her face up to her husband's in eager delight. 'Oh Henry! Is this not the most perfectly happy moment? To be standing here, finally, after everything that has happened! I cannot believe we are truly married!' She squeezed his arm. 'Now all the delay seems merely nothing at all! I am so happy I can hardly blink in case it should all be a dream!'

The young people had been forced to wait a year before being sanctioned to marry by General Tilney. A year earlier, Catherine had been invited by the General to stay at Northanger Abbey. Supposing Catherine to be the future recipient of a large endowment upon the demise of the Allens, a wealthy and childless couple who were on intimate terms with the family, the scheming General had been bitterly disappointed. As soon as it became known that no such endowment upon Catherine had ever been contemplated by Mr Allen, the General had angrily stood in the way of his son's union, accusing Catherine of posing as an heiress to lure Henry in. He had verily sent her away in disgrace, cast his son off almost as immediately, and refused to give his consent to a marriage. Perhaps any other two people might have flaunted parental authority and run away to be married, but Henry and Catherine, having strong characters but even stronger moral principles, had been resolved to part and wait until such time as the General would soften, or to discover if providence was their friend.

It had taken a full year and much patience, devotion, and surreptitious letter writing on the part of the young people to endure the separation, but on the sudden marriage of Eleanor Tilney, Henry's older sister, to a young man of considerable fortune, the General was thrown into a temporary fit of good humour, and in due course they received his begrudging consent to marry. And so, after a year of delay, Henry and Catherine had married at Fullerton, and in order to cause Henry no delay in returning to his duties, they had spurned the new fashion of taking an extensive bridal tour and set off immediately after the wedding breakfast for Woodston.

Her husband being sincerely attached to his new wife, and allowing *almost* anything she exclaimed to be exactly so, now smiled his agreement down at her. 'After all the delays occasioned by my father, I can only agree wholeheartedly with you that there has been no material harm to our future felicity; and even if I cannot own to being the dreamer that you are, Cathy, I submit that if *you* consider we are come to Woodston to be happy forever after, then I shall consider it my husbandly duty to comply.' He smiled down at her and took her hand. 'And we will indeed be so, if you will only come inside rather than keep me standing outside my own house in the cold!'

Catherine had the grace to blush a little and laugh at herself. 'Sorry, my love. Shall we go inside then? Oh, here the servants are come out to greet us! I do hope they will still like me now that I am to give them their orders!'

Before Henry could protest that of course they all did like her already, very much indeed, the large door had given way to a half dozen servants, who had made haste to greet the new mistress of the parsonage. Two young males, and four females, two of whom were older than Catherine, and all of whom had varying degrees of welcome on their countenances, lined up obediently to greet the new-made Mrs and Mr Tilney.

Catherine's heart fluttered. But on the arm of her husband, she felt brave enough to advance with him and be made to hear their various civilities. When Henry stopped at the top of the line, in front of an older woman, he said, 'Of course, you have met Mrs Poulter, my housekeeper. She will be a great help to you, I am sure,' he added kindly.

Mrs Poulter was middle-aged woman of hostile aspect. Her long devotion to Henry's interests and to Woodston had caused her to be filled with suspicion at the prospect of anyone taking her place in the ranks of the Woodston empire. She had not warmed to Catherine, not even after two official visits to Woodston as Henry's betrothed.

But Catherine was gratified when the woman curtsied and said stiffly, 'Mrs Tilney. Welcome back to Woodston parsonage, Ma'am. May I offer my congratulations to you both?'

As Catherine contemplated in astonishment the novelty of being addressed as "Ma'am", Henry smiled. 'You may and we thank you, Mrs Poulter.'

The woman's chilly eyes barely warmed as they alighted on Catherine. 'I hope you will be very happy here, Mrs Tilney. The fire is lit in the drawing room, if you would please to go straight in, or if you wish I can have you shown to your apartments.'

Catherine, much surprised to hear she would have her own apartments and wondering why she had not seen them before or knew such a thing existed at Woodston, exclaimed, 'Oh, how delightful Mrs Poulter! I did not expect to have apartments. Indeed, the house is large enough, I imagine, only I did not notice a suite of rooms upstairs before when I have come to visit...' she trailed off, as there was silence from the housekeeper.

Henry took her arm again. 'I think Mrs Poulter meant only a bedroom, Cathy, which we shall both share of course, plus a small dressing room for my own use which you have not seen, and a little sitting parlour adjoining it which I never use and I thought might delight you to sit in as it looks out over the orchard and woods.'

Catherine's face suffused with pink, both at her own *faux pas*, and in sudden modesty at Henry's mentioning of the bedroom they would share. 'Of course, how silly it was of me to think there was an entire suite of rooms, after I have seen over the whole house. It all sounds perfectly delightful, I am sure!'

She had not realised that Henry's own chamber had such a thing as a small dressing room and an adjoining sitting room, but then, she had only dared to peep inside Henry's bedroom once, the last time she had been invited to visit, with her sister Sarah for chaperone.

Then she remembered too, the few moments on that same visit, when she had been left alone downstairs to amuse herself. She had been enticed by her own curiosity to try a door, hidden in the dim hallway, which had a mysterious look about it. The door had not budged, being quite locked, and she had been forced to conclude her exploration with a guilty start when Mrs Poulter had come up suddenly behind her and sharply enquired if there 'was anything she could help the young miss with?' Catherine had at once dissembled and retreated hastily into the garden, but the incident had incited her interest in the mysterious door.

Perhaps this was the door to the rooms Henry had mentioned? But no, that door had been on the ground floor and Henry's rooms on the second floor. But she would soon make sense of the house, she was sure. Catherine now clasped Henry's arm more firmly and ventured, 'I *am* a little tired—perhaps I should go to our room, my love—I should not wish to trouble Mrs Poulter.' Mrs Poulter, noted Catherine, made a remarkable effort not to smirk. Her heart sank further.

'It is no trouble, Mrs Tilney, and beside that the master has immediate parish business to attend.' The older woman turned to Henry. 'Your curate Mr. Stevens is here, Sir, and awaits you in the study.'

Henry turned to Catherine. 'I am sorry, my darling. Can you forgive my absence just for a little while and Mrs Poulter will take you to our room and to a good fire. You look chilled. And not a little fatigued.' He dropped a kiss on her forehead. 'Rest and I will come to you very soon, I promise!'

Before Catherine had had time to give her assent or reject the proposal, Henry had turned on his heel and gone away, leaving Catherine to the mercy of the eyes of Mrs Poulter. She withered a little beneath them.

'If you'll follow me, Ma'am.'

Catherine was grateful to be left alone in Henry's great master bedroom a few minutes later, where a fire blazed cheerfully. She watched the disappearing back of Mrs Poulter with great relief. Goodness! She had only been "Mrs Tilney" for less than a day and already she was feeling as if she might have entered Woodston unprepared for the taxing of her every nerve! But she had Henry and she would soon find her place and feel less intimidated by the good Mrs Poulter, she thought. Putting off her bonnet, gloves and spencer, she threw them down haphazardly over a large cushiony chair which fronted the fireplace. It was not as if she had never entered the house before, she thought, and she was familiar enough with the rooms and their placements. It was not Northanger, with its maze of staircases, back passages and hidden doors! No, this was Woodston, cosy and cheerful and welcoming, and if Henry was beside her, she thought she might enjoy no greater felicity than to live in a simple style, in a home which could house no secrets, and harbour no misery such as Northanger had!

She went to the window, and gazed down momentarily upon the garden, but as quickly turned away and went to the door to see if her bags were being brought up. Ascertaining that no footsteps were heard as yet, she turned back to the room and this time, being unable to avoid the point any longer, forced herself to look at the huge, white-dressed bed which dominated the chamber. It was not as if she was a child, she thought, but even with that thought her colour rose and she found herself nervously contemplating the image in her mind of herself and Henry, sleeping there together, talking, and doing things she understood to require no conversation at all!

These thoughts brought a pink to her cheeks, and a quiver to her insides. Mama had told her all that she had seen fit regarding the producing of offspring, and if that good woman had left anything out, Catherine had been an avid student of romantic novels long enough to understand the details. She longed for Henry to take her in his arms, just as the novels described, there to find the mysterious bliss of which they spoke, but she could hardly help being just a little nervous, all the same!

Henry's room was as it had ever been on the last occasion of her chance viewing. It was pleasant, warm and cheerful, with large comfortable chairs before a fire, and two high chests full of drawers. An end wall gave way to lovely ornate cupboard roomy enough for more gowns than she had ever owned, and there were some modest, pretty landscapes hung on three of the four walls. Another table sported a large pitcher and basin, where Henry must carry out his ablutions of a morning. Her heart skipped strangely as she imagined her new husband, half dressed, stripped to the waist, soaping himself liberally, and she tried to imagine herself doing the same next to him. How did a married couple share the pitcher and basin? How would she cover herself, and what if she wished to bathe? At home she always bathed in a tub before her own fire!

Although her mama had given her the advice and admonitions which every young girl receives upon her marriage if they have mothers that care for them, the answers to these lesser mysteries had not been explained to her. Nor had these finer details, even with all her reading, been gleaned from any of the modest novels she had poured over all her life. But she had long ago given up the childish imaginings which such reading had aroused in her; she would never forget the lessons learned at Northanger last summer. Then she had been a child; now, she thought to herself, she was a woman, a wife, and more grown-up than she had ever felt in her life. Sharing a bed chamber, and all that this entailed, she welcomed, and if Mrs Poulter's slight unwelcoming attitude had unsettled her at all, she would by-and-by have Henry to cheer her up again! She went to sit upon the end of the bed to await her trunks and when Henry did finally find himself free to come upstairs to attend his new bride, it was to find her curled fast asleep at the end of the big bed, the lemon and rose sarcenet gown she had been married in that morning a foil for the glossy dark hair which was fetchingly spread out upon the crisp white counterpane.

Two

Four weeks of marriage supplied Catherine with all the delights and comforts that she felt were necessary for perfect domestic felicity. Each day was spent in the company of her husband, whose doting smiles and singular attentions supplied her with all the proof she had ever wanted of his devotion to her happiness. One day he would surprise her with a picnic in the grounds, the next with a visit to a nearby pleasure spot, where he would explain to her what constituted a perfect landscape, or how a watermill was able to thresh wheat which made up the bread she was eating. She drank in his every word, an eager student, and just as eager for the improvement of her own understanding as he was for her entertainment. They rode together daily, Henry having purchased for her a lovely grey mare of just the right height and temperament to suit its rider.

Catherine had been in raptures. 'I shall call her Cleo, after Queen Cleopatra, you see, for she is just as pretty as I imagine Cleopatra to have been!' she exclaimed as she stroked the animal's velvety forehead.

Henry had laughed and given her no argument since she had been making an effort to read more widely, and it had been he himself who had given her *A History of Ancient Egypt,* at her wide-eyed insistence that she would 'indeed read every word; it was not as though she were still a young girl with no interest in serious, adult subjects!'

It had only been a year since she had professed a dislike of history and dismissed it as being a tedious duty to read, but since she had become engaged to Henry she had tuned over a new leaf and determined upon a course of self-improvement by reading more widely. Her parents had by no means been frugal with the education of their children; rather, Catherine had been a very poor student indeed, and had been hard pressed to study when all she had wanted was to frolic and run with her brothers or bury her head in a novel when she ought to have been reading her French grammar.

She had also determined to be at her piano again, having long since abandoned that barbaric instrument of torture for the pleasure of novels. And she wished very much to become competent in drawing and painting, to tackle history with a new zest, to improve her French and she hoped, study a little botany or philosophy, whichever was easier to understand, she thought. Armed with mental images of her own dedication and studiousness and anticipating the pleasant compliments her efforts were sure to evoke from Henry, she was vastly pleased with her scheme. She was full ready to embark upon it, too, for of all the things in the world she wished most for Henry to be proud of her as his wife.

In this regard she had Eleanor to emulate, for Henry's sister was all Catherine herself aspired to be: accomplished in many disciplines, generally clever, elegant and modest, while at the same time mature, and carrying herself with a quiet, self-assured confidence.

Catherine had therefore made a beginning by begging Henry to choose for her a list of books by which she would improve her knowledge, and she had even purchased for herself a painting easel and some brushes and paints, and a new grammar in French which, with its little amusing drawings of objects, — '*un pomme, un cheval* ' — did not look too grim and serious.

A month's advancement had also taught Catherine more about married life than she had ever read about in novels. She had been given entry through that doorway into which only married ladies are invited to pass. She had come to accept the non-verbal proofs of Henry's devotion; they had shared a bed, she had bathed in a long tub before the fire, in full view of his appreciative glances, and subjected herself to his ministrations when he insisted on washing her hair. He had kissed her and taken his delight in her, until she, laughing and crying at the same time, had begged for a little rest. She had barely blushed after the first night, so comfortable and happy she was in the warmth of Henry's affections, and when her clear blue eyes opened to meet his own hazel ones in the mornings, she had only smiles and delight in finding herself still living a dream from which she never wished to awaken.

The only shadow which occasionally disturbed this scene of domestic contentment was her nervousness around Mrs Poulter, and her inexperience as mistress of her own establishment. Mrs Poulter had been patient with the new Mrs Tilney, explaining every aspect of the household's running in more detail than Catherine could hope to take in and the older woman made much show about deferring to Catherine's judgement and taste when the day's menu or the question of how many flower arrangements were to adorn the parlour was to tax Catherine's sad housekeeping skills. Even so, Catherine could not help the nervous little skip of her heartbeat when she rounded a corner and found the woman standing silhouetted in one of the windows as if she had been standing there, as still as a statue, for some time, as if waiting on purpose to frighten her, or when the woman came up suddenly behind Catherine without a sound and made her start.

The housekeeper was polite, always, and yet there was still something of disapproval in her light grey eyes, and although Catherine tried to converse, she gave up after few stammered sentences. She began the habit of deferring to Mrs Poulter the decisions for which she herself had been solicited to give.

'I don't know what it is,' she had explained to Henry one evening as they sat up together in the large white bed, 'I cannot but feel so— so inadequate around her. I feel that she thinks I must be a very silly young bride who knows nothing at all about keeping a house! And it is true!' she added sadly.

Henry had kissed her lingeringly then lifted a curl of stray hair away from Catherine's forehead.

'My darling Kitty, as a clergyman it is my duty to live modestly, and it is true that I cannot be seen to have a greater number of servants than any other family in the village, but we are not as hard up as to make it necessary for my wife to undertake those tasks which perhaps your own mother needed to do herself. You need not try to take on everything at once, you know.'

'True, but I should like to know as much as possible about the running of the house so as not to appear ridiculous! Mrs Poulter thinks me a child, I am sure!'

Henry consoled her with a kiss. 'Then allow Mrs Poulter to show you how everything is done and learn from her. It takes courage and patience to learn something new, especially if it is something which does not come naturally.'

'Cannot *you* show me?'

Henry smiled kindly. 'I cannot be here all the time, Cathy. I have naturally taken a small leave from some of my duties to ensure you are settled in at Woodston. Next month, however, I shall have to be more and more from home to attend to parish matters. Mrs P will have to be your guide in these things. She is long used to running the house for me, and now she must give way to your authority; I daresay it must not be easy for one who is so used to running everything. Perhaps she is taking a little longer to adapt, but she has been very kind to you, and I am sure you will come to rely upon her advice in every domestic matter. You need not be shy of her, you know, she is as harmless a creature as your own dear mama!'

Catherine made a little moue. 'I know you are right, for you are always right, only I do want her to like me. Oh, my heavens! Henry!'

Henry had already begun to silence her with his lips and for a while the topic was abandoned in favour of pleasanter matters.

~ ~ * ~ ~

Catherine, for all her faults, was humble enough to acknowledge them, and in seeking her own self-improvement she truly felt that she would be forming herself into a better wife for Henry. She observed the servants as much as she could, and asked many questions, until Mrs Poulter chanced to find her in conversation with Jane one morning and chastised the poor girl for indolence and shirking her work. After this, Catherine was careful not to prevent the servants from carrying out their work and only observed and tried to glean some idea of the workings of the house from a distance.

She did not neglect her mind, and dutifully picked up *A History of Ancient Egypt*, or *Kings and Queens of England*, almost every day, reading at least a few pages until she could not absorb any more. Then she would take her paints and pencils outside and try to make sketches of the house and grounds. Painting and drawing she found less tedious than reading history, so she had more success with her art than she did with recalling which queen was beheaded in which year and which king responsible. She recalled Henry's tutoring of her a year ago, when they had been at Beecham Cliff in Bath, when they had discussed what made a scene picturesque. Now she laboured to add in the right amount of foreground and background, and to ensure her focal point was clear, although she was seldom sure she had gotten it right.

Henry, noting her efforts and being very much flattered by this desire to please, promised her a tutor. 'If you really mean to become more accomplished at drawing, then I shall get you Longstaff, Eleanor's old master; he is living only two miles from here, and I am sure he would come once a week to look over what you have done. But Catherine, you know you don't need to be able to draw and paint, or speak French to make me happy? My parishioners hardly expect you to hold a conversation in French with them! If you are so good as to sometimes deliver them some game from the estate or butter from our dairy, I think you will be as successful a clergyman's wife as any other!'

'I know,' she replied plaintively, 'but I so want to make up for my laziness as a girl, to be a good wife — one of whom you can be proud! I may not,' she added seriously, 'be very good at housekeeping, but I can at least be as accomplished as Eleanor — it would be shocking thing indeed if your parishioners were to discover I cannot even pick up a needle and darn your socks, or play something simple on the pianoforte, or paint a scene tolerably well! They would think me a great oaf, indeed!'

Henry laughed. 'Dearest creature, I hardly think being able to play one of Mozart's sonatas on the piano will further my career as a sermonizer, but by all means shape yourself into as accomplished a young lady as you like — I am quite excessively love with you already, and your not speaking French or understanding the difference between the sublime and the picturesque will not make me love you any the less, you know!'

Nevertheless, at Catherine's insistence the painting master was summoned in due course, and Catherine spent a not unpleasant two or three hours each week improving her painting skills under the watchful eye of Mr Longstaff, with the hopes that, in time, she might manage one or two little watercolours to give Henry.

Three

I must venture, dear reader, to interrupt my tale, in order to give an account of this Mr Longstaff, for he will, as you will soon find, be of significance in relation to the evolution of Catherine and Henry's future nuptial happiness.

Mr Charles Longstaff was an excessively well-looking young man, of around one or two-and thirty. He had trained in law after being educated by a tutor, but having a tolerable talent for art, he had soon abandoned law in order to dedicate himself to this alternate vocation. Finding that, after ten years labour and few commissions of note, he had made naught but a very modest success in England, he then determined to teach painting, and spent half his time teaching, and the other half of his year in London enjoying the amusements to be found there. He did not want for fortune, since he had been left by his father a sum which was enough to sufficiently fund a tolerable living, and only taught painting in order to exercise his talent in the only way left to him. He was however, possessed of a good education, tolerably informed conversation, and a charm which came easily. He was the kind of gentleman who can never go into a room unheeded, and in indeed, can leave it neither, without every female attached and unattached alike, looking after him wistfully. It was whispered behind the spread fans of many giggling young ladies of his acquaintance, that he 'filled out his britches admirably' and that he was a person 'of the most striking appearance.'

For all that he was one of the most well-looking gentlemen in England, it might justifiably be noted that such a specimen of good looks is rarely united with excellent manners, but the case was not so with Mr Charles Longstaff. His manners were discovered by all his acquaintance to be impeccable, refined and pleasing, and he had all those sincere and flattering little ways which never failed to attach ladies to him almost immediately. Coupled with a happy appearance of modesty and a perfectly genteel indifference of address when he was presented to this swooning lady or that, it was thought he was so unaware of his own attractions as to make even more him even more capable of warmly attaching the proudest and coolest of females. But he was not of a mind to marry, and beyond satisfying his carnal instinct with those women of easy virtue who would not expect marriage, he was inclined to consider it was his God-given duty to flirt with and tease those young ladies of breeding whom he met, and then to move on without looking back.

Needless to say, he left behind him a number of broken hearts everywhere he chanced to go, and but for the certainty that to boast would undermine his reputation as excessively modest, he had learned to feign astonishment, and declare that 'he had never been aware of a single one of them paying him any peculiarity of address, and he had certainly given no conscious encouragement.'

Such was the *public* character of Mr Longstaff, and none but the most astute of persons, older and wiser, would see anything sinister in so open and pleasing a gentleman. There were some gentlemen among his acquaintance who did not find his charms as natural as the females in his company might have done, but these only smiled at his artfulness, for to flatter and please and to break a few hearts, they said to themselves, is the just right of man. Do we consider Mr Longstaff to be a rake, then? Why, that is for you to judge, dear reader. He was never called one in his life, but perhaps Henry might have called him a scoundrel and reprobate, had he but comprehended Longstaff's character more intimately.

At any rate, on a fine Tuesday afternoon, a month or so after Henry and Catherine were married, Mr Charles Longstaff entered the village of Woodston with no immediate idea of doing any mischief. He was sanguine indeed. Mr Henry Tilney was known to him as the brother of the very pretty Miss Tilney, now Lady

Torrington, whom he had once admired very much. When Henry Tilney had written and requested his services at Woodston, he had agreed to teach the new Mrs Tilney out of a regard for his former pupil. A married lady rarely stirred his interest much, since, quite apart from the tedium of manoeuvring around the jealous husbands, he was convinced of their being excessively dull once they were married. He had no interest in conversing with them on children, chickens or servants, although it was amusing sometimes to see if they would respond to his flirting.

But Mrs Tilney had at once caught his eye. Normally she would not have possessed charms enough to tempt him, for she was not beautiful at all, only tolerably pretty, but her youthful prettiness and air of uncertainty, combined with a certain boredom he had been lately labouring under, presented to him a challenge something in the manner of low-hanging fruit. The lady being married, of course, was likely to put him off, but being only recently made a married woman, she must have no children, which left only the chickens and servants to be on guard against. However, on conversing with her from the start, he found Mrs Tilney was charmingly innocent, and less disposed to talk as to ask many questions and hear with a charming eagerness his replies. In short, she was such a devoted student that his vanity was flattered enough to render her appealing when he was in the mood for a little fun. And when she had let slip that her husband was soon to be often from home, he had idly decided that life had been dull enough of late, and that perhaps a few months of visits here would afford him some entertainment after all.

It pains me to say, dear reader, that an unsuspecting Henry had shaken his hand as an old acquaintance, and had handed his wife over to handsome Mr Longstaff without compunction. But when one is not paying attention, one must expect misfortune, as we shall soon discover. The lessons were begun, and Catherine was from the first moment in a fluster in Mr Longstaff's presence, although his amusing remarks and his patience with her efforts soon put her *almost* at her ease.

There was a certain studied charm in his manners and address to Catherine which made her very aware of herself, and when his hand casually brushed against hers, or he stood very close behind her, she noticed her hand shook just a little, and her heart beat just a little faster than normal.

All this she put down to nerves, and chided herself for being so silly, even while his knowing smile unnerved her if she were to glance up suddenly and find him watching her. It was just his way she thought, and after a while, she became used to his presence and when he wasn't teasing her, she enjoyed his conversation. He was not as well-informed as Henry, she thought, but he did not lecture her in the same manner. He answered her questions readily and without scorn, talked at length of his travels, asked for her opinion numerous times, and on occasion he even laughed at something she said, although she had not meant to be amusing. It was pleasant to be treated as an adult, and she began to see that Henry's constant lecturing, as informative as it was, was perhaps only one way to learn about the world.

In mentioning to Eleanor the addition of her old art tutor to Cathy's weekly activities, her sister-in law had written back a rather mysterious reply, in which Catherine was exhorted to 'take all care, my dear sister, that you do not allow yourself to be taken in by those who seek to hide their true natures.'

Cathy could take no rational meaning from this comment, and passed it off as Eleanor's being confused, or out of sorts.

After a time she became used to Mr Longstaff's presence quite close behind her as she worked, and to watch as he corrected her errors and show her how certain brush strokes might create a myriad of different impressions. He was as flattering to her efforts as Henry was not. While Henry would, when he came across her in the garden, tease her with comments such as, 'What a handsome elephant you have made in the foreground!' and 'Is that a tree or a tall bonnet issuing from that riverbank?', Longstaff commended her efforts with effusive praise.

While Catherine was well aware than her pencil was her greatest deficiency and was modest enough to know flattery when it was applied, she was grateful for the kind praise, even while she sighed and tried not to blot her flowers into shapeless blobs. Despite Mr Longstaff's kind flattery, she had to admit that under his tutelage her paintings and drawings were slowly improving. At pains in her labours, she finished each session sure her head would surely burst from all the advice and admonishments, but as unindustrious as she was in most pursuits, even her mother would have been proud to see her stick to her resolve to become a properly accomplished lady.

~ ~ * ~ ~

And so proceeded Catherine's scheme to improve herself. Besides practising her painting and drawing, the poor pianoforte in the drawing room was laboured at frequently in the first weeks of marriage but, I am sad to admit, less frequently as time went by. Music requires much of those who wish to master the art of making it, and poor Catherine, as eager as she was to improve herself for her husband's sake, could not overcome her dislike for perseverance in subjects which she found too difficult. The French grammar went much the same way, as soon as simple nouns and objects gave way to lessons on conjugating verbs, but she did find that botany interested her. For a wedding gift she had received a little book on the topic from Eleanor, and on thumbing through the first few pages, she had found the little drawings of flowers and leaves interesting enough that it was no labour to continue. She applied herself to the subject and became almost knowledgeable when tested by Henry on what she had learned.

Thus passed the first few weeks of marriage, with both parties eager for the happiness of the other, and so happy they were generally that nothing in the choice of conversation topics other than the certainty of their own felicity was needed when they were not too busy with other, less conversational activities.

Mrs Poulter continued to run the house, and to consult Catherine on the menus and the number of chickens and pigs to be sent to market, although there seemed to be a remarkable number of confusing details to be discussed, and trying to keep up with Mrs Poulter's expositions made her head ache. Besides this, being inattentive to much of her mother's tuition on the topics of either housekeeping or pig-keeping, Catherine could add very little of her own preferences to the housekeeper's recommendations. She tried to learn, and indeed she did gain a modicum of knowledge by default; from observing the servants sometimes in the yard, she knew which of the girls milked Betsy the cow, where the grain to feed the chickens was kept, and how to scatter it in the enclosure so as to be able to collect the eggs while the hens were all busy scratching for food. But all this could not help her advise Mrs Poulter on whether partridge or pheasant were preferred when Rev. Holbrook was to come for dinner, and she could hardly say if she wanted Jenny to bring down the good dinner set for Mr and Mrs Tilney's use, or to remain using the second-best plate.

Four

Henry, devoted to his parish and his duty as much as he was devoted to his wife, had now begun to be more absent from home. Four days a week he would leave on horseback after breakfast and return only in time for a late dinner around five o' clock. When he was at home, he was often in his study writing sermons or dealing with his curate. Catherine was always more nervous when Henry was not at home, fearing to come upon the intimidating person of Mrs Poulter unawares, or to be caught, just as guiltily, being indolent in the drawing room. She took to staying in her room and reading, but when she knew Mrs Poulter was out on errands, she spent some of the time wandering the house.

Woodston was not so large as to become lost in it, but not so small as to easily become tired of it. Catherine had curiously explored the third floor and had discovered two rooms which led off the servants landing, and which were unused. Seeing as one had a fireplace built in, she went to ask Mrs Poulter if she might use it for herself as a place to paint when it was too cold out of doors. She had become almost enthusiastic for the past-time and had even produced a tolerable painting which Henry had kindly pronounced, 'Capital, very pretty!' Spurred on by such effusive praise, Catherine had tried very hard to improve by frequent practise.

When she put her proposition to Mrs Poulter, however, that lady eyed her with a steely glare. 'Those rooms are next to the maids' rooms, Ma'am. It would not do for the mistress of the house to be spending time upstairs hobnobbing with the servants and such,' she admonished coolly. 'Not to mention the servants could hardly be themselves in their own rooms if they knew you were only next door. I am sure you see that, Ma'am.'

'Why, yes, of course, I would not wish to disturb Jane and Emily,' uttered Catherine miserably. 'I— I did not mean any harm, but I only wanted—'

'If you be wanting a place for your painting, I can just as surely clear a space in the private parlour which adjoins the Master's room, Mrs Tilney. Mr Tilney meant for you to use it for your own purposes. You have hardly been in it, Ma'am,' she added accusingly.

'Of course — thankyou, Mrs Poulter, you are very kind. How silly of me not to think of that — indeed I am sorry to have troubled you with it. It's just that I do so love the downstairs drawing room — it is such a pretty room and the view of the little cottages and the apple trees is so pleasant —' she trailed off, rose suffusing her cheeks.

'Tis no trouble, Ma'am,' replied Mrs Poulter with a long suffering look in her eye.

Catherine had retreated, chastised enough to feel quite low-spirited, but it was only later, when she chanced to go along towards the kitchen and overhear the voice of Mrs Poulter talking to Cook in such a manner as to make Catherine blush with vexation, that she began to resent Mrs Poulter's presence.

'...entirely unseemly, for the wife of a parson to be painting pictures next door to the servant's rooms, when she ought to be out and about paying charitable visits to the sick, or doing flowers for the chapel! Goodness knows, I know they are only just married but she will have to learn quickly the life of a clergyman's wife is not perhaps what she were used to at home! La! Thinking she could just waltz in and make herself at home in the upstairs! It would have put Emily to no end of trouble, to be making up a fire in the room every day! That girl has enough work to do without tending extra fires!'

Catherine had crept from the door feeling quite ashamed. Although Henry had encouraged her to settle in before she took up the expected duties of a clergyman's wife, she was conscious that she had delayed such activities longer than could be warranted, and Mrs Poulter's comments shamed her. She would talk to Henry directly about making visits to the poor. As for the use of a room for painting, she would make do with outdoors, and from that time forward she would always ask Henry first, before she did anything.

Not that there was much she wished to change, for all-in-all Woodston parsonage was as pretty and well-furnished on the inside as any fine house she had been in. When she had come for her second visit to the parsonage and Henry had given her license to change anything she liked when they were married, she had declared the house perfect then, and that every room was just as she would have had it, the staff all perfectly kind to her, and that she would not alter a thing for all the world. But now, she wished, just a very little, that Mrs Poulter might resign her position as housekeeper, so that Catherine might not suffer the injustice of always feeling guilty under the woman's glance.

$$\sim \; \sim \; * \; \sim \; \sim$$

Another incident which occurred the very next day also made her wish the woman would give up her position, although it made her feel very evil indeed to wish for such a thing. Catherine had been wandering along the downstairs hallway which led to the kitchen and she came again upon the door almost hidden in the dim hallway, which was locked on her last visit. Trying the handle guiltily, she reasoned thus: 'I am the mistress of the house now. Surely I can go into which ever rooms I wish, and as mistress I really ought to know what is behind this door!' Then the door gave way to her will, and she was astonished to find a stairway which led down into the depths of the house.

A year earlier, when she had been invited to be a guest at Northanger Abbey, Catherine had allowed a vivid imagination to lead her down a path of shame and contrition. Allowing her reading to have had too great a power over her mind, she had come to expect all the horrors of *The Monk,* or *The Mysteries of Udolpho* to be found at Northanger. Indeed, she had even foolishly attributed violent acts to the General, believing him at one time capable of murder. After she had been severely set down by Henry, and suffered the wretchedness of humiliation and disgrace, she had from that moment sworn off the romantic novels of her youth and vowed to become a vastly more sensible girl.

However, for all Catherine's resolve to never again be accused of folly and misguidedness as she had in the past, for all her determination never to let her fancies carry away her reason, she was helpless against the picture before her. Here was a stairwell, for all intents and purposed banned to her entry by a dour housekeeper, leading mysteriously downstairs, when she had had no inkling, no notion of any such thing existing at cheerful Woodston; even despite her resolve to reject the influences of Mrs Radcliffe, it was more than her imagination could resist. Suddenly the urge to explore was her first, most pressing object, but, alas for poor Catherine, who had not heard the footsteps behind her, the very person whom Catherine would have most wished *not* to meet with at that moment, was the very person whom she found standing behind her.

'Mrs Poulter!' exclaimed she, reddening at once, which must have served, she thought afterward, only to increase the appearance of guilt. 'I— I only wanted to find out what was behind this door — I had not realized there was a lower floor —'

'There is a basement, Ma'am, the wine cellar — and very dark and musty it is, I must say, and nothing at all down there of interest excepting the master's liquor. You will only ruin your pretty white gown if you try to go below. I daresay you have better things to be doing at any rate, than getting grubby and banging your head on old beams and what not!'

'I — yes, of course. I am quite sure I don't need to go down there at all, I only wondered where it went to. Thankyou Mrs Poulter.' She closed the door again and watched in dismay as Mrs Poulter stepped forward and turned the big silver key in the lock and pocketed it.

Perhaps her dismay was obvious for the housekeeper said coolly, 'It is mostly kept locked, Ma'am, so that the servants don't fall down the steps — them being old and perhaps not as safe as they ought to be.'

For a moment Catherine blinked. 'Oh, you mean the stairs! I thought you meant Jane or Jenny! — but perhaps then we ought to make the stairs more secure?' she added in some alarm. 'I am *sure* Mr Tilney would wish it! — if that is the case, then please see that the steps are reinforced — or whatever it is they need, Mrs Poulter

— if you will be so kind!' she added almost apologetically and somewhat astonished at her own bravery in giving an actual order. 'I would not like to hear of anybody falling down them!'

'Certainly ma'am,' replied Mrs Poulter blandly. She turned away, taking the key with her.

~ ~ * ~ ~

Catherine had informed Henry of the incident when he had come home, but he had taken Mrs Poulter's side. 'I couldn't have you falling down any steps, my love, as curious a creature as you are. You must not on any account go down. It is only a musty old cellar, after all. Have you never heard that "God fashioned Hell for the Inquisitive"?'

Catherine had been hurt that Henry would so quickly take his housekeeper's side, and felt quite misunderstood, but she did not say so and only determined to avoid Mrs Poulter as much as she could. Why the old housekeeper was so set against her going down there, she could not guess, but surely there must be something in the cellar she did not want Catherine to see; her story about the stairs being unsafe seemed so contrived as to be quite made up on the spot, Catherine mused.

And so Catherine, vexed that she had not been able to see for herself the hidden rooms below the house, and resenting the housekeeper for what she felt was overly officious behaviour, had wished, for the second time, that perhaps Mrs Poulter might suddenly have a sister take very ill and be forced to resign her position, or that the woman herself might fall down the forbidden stairs and break — but no, that was unchristian and Catherine was not so evil as to wish harm upon another person. Still, as much as she admonished herself, her curiosity did wish to discover the rooms below, and although she had come a long way from allowing absurd fears and fantastic imaginings to persuade her into unreasonable behaviour, she was quite wild to explore the cellar which had for all intents and purposed been banned to her.

"She was quite wild to explore."

Five

Catherine found that she was becoming increasingly restless when Henry was absent, and Henry was becoming increasingly absent as marriages, baptism and funerals, estate affairs, and sermon-writing returned him to normal life. She had at first been dismayed to learn how occupied Henry was on a daily basis. 'Must you go out so often?' she had asked Henry. 'Perhaps I can accompany you — or you can read your sermons to me to practise them!'

Henry had been kind but firm. 'I have been rather neglectful of the estate and my parish, Cathy, and now I feel that we have had honeymoon enough; you must fortify yourself to really becoming a parson's wife! When I am absent, there are so many things for you to do — I can begin by asking Mr Stevens to give you a list of the sick and poor families who will by now be expecting a visit. You can take Jenny with you, if you wish it. In the meantime, you have your reading and your own pursuits to keep you occupied when I must be away. And Cleo must be exercised!'

'Well, yes, of course,' she had replied hesitantly. 'Only I am used to being in company with so many brothers and sisters, and it can feel very strange to be here on my own so much.'

'You must make yourself as useful as you can and begin to make charity visits. Mrs Poulter told me she found you lurking in the kitchen the other day, of all places, distracting cook from her duties. There are so many things to occupy you, my dear, that you should not need to bother the servants for occupation or company.'

Catherine, feeling for the second time quite misunderstood by her own dear Henry, was silent, feeling guilty for complaining of his absence at all. She resolved to be more at her wifely duties, and to do as Henry suggested and visit the sick. She had never on her own done such a thing before, but at home she had helped Mama make up suet puddings and wrap them up, and had even accompanied her on occasion to deliver baskets to the invalid and poor. It would do, for now, to keep her mind occupied when Henry was not at home. Mrs Poulter would have no more opportunity to complain of Catherine lurking in the kitchen and disturbing the servants!

So she did just that, taking Jenny with her, and found visiting the parish was not as imposing a task as she had imagined it, for the poor family she had gone to was humble enough to be glad to see her. She felt very much a parson's wife as she handed over a loaf of bread and some butter and milk from Woodston's own dairy, and found that there was a great deal of pleasure in giving.

Jenny, a stout woman of around five-and-thirty, was well-disposed to talk, and Catherine found that she was a font of information about the families hereabouts, having been in service at the parsonage since she was married and at Northanger before that. Although she chattered a little much for Catherine's ears, Catherine was grateful to have company on her first visit to represent her husband. Feeling she had really done her first real duty as a clergyman's wife, Catherine was well pleased with herself when she returned home.

'You've made poor Mrs Lowe happier than I have seen her for a while, Ma'am,' chattered Jenny as they turned into the garden gate by the side of the house. 'Lonely without her husband, she is. And six mouths to feed! La! I always thought it about time Mr Tilney got someone to help with charity visits. Lor! Miss Parkhurst would not have made a very good parson's wife, with her airs and ways, though she was handsome enough —' she stopped short, colouring. 'Pardon me, Miss, I was thinking of someone else I knew a long time ago, just then. At any rate its ever so lovely to see Woodston parsonage with a lady in it! A man of the cloth can't never do 'is job proper without a Mrs, that's what my George says, and I reckon he's right. I best get in now Ma'am, before Mrs P comes looking for me!'

Catherine was astonished. 'But who is Miss Parkhurst?'

The woman bit her lip anxiously. 'Why, don't you know, Ma'am? Well, I don't know as it's my place to say... but I suppose there can be no harm in you knowing the story,' she added doubtfully.

Catherine, now assailed by the strongest curiosity and astonishment replied, 'No, indeed, no harm at all! Do go on!'

'Well, Ma'am, it's only that Mr Tilney was keen on the young lady for a time — it was near ten or so years ago mind, before he first took orders and got the living here at Woodston. He must have been about eighteen years old, Ma'am. What a fine young man he was too, ever so well-looking and always so polite and well mannered. Well, here was Miss Parkhurst, the only daughter of Colonel Parkhurst. She were a sweet young thing, very pretty, and only fifteen or sixteen years, I'd reckon. She were a guest at Northanger several times, I believe; her father were a friend of the General's, see? We all thought Mr Henry might ask her to marry him, even though they was so young, since they was ever so keen on each other. But then, she weren't no favourite of the General for his son on account of her having no fortune, Ma'am. I don't know what happened after that, I seem to recall that suddenly it was all over with them, and there were a dreadful lot of talk over it upstairs, and a bit of a to-do, but I don't rightly know the whole story. But after that Colonel Parkhurst never came again to the Abbey. My George thinks it was all over the lack of money, and the General's not approving the match, but that were a long time ago, Ma'am and nothing to regard now, I am sure!'

Catherine, who had never thought of Henry's being attached to anyone before he met her, had nothing to reply, such as was her astonishment.

'Are you quite well Ma'am?' asked Jenny anxiously. 'You've gone quite pale! I am not sure it were right of me to tell you after all! I do hope you won't tell the master; I am very sorry if I did wrong.'

'I am quite well, I thank you. I was only surprised because I had not known of it, but all persons, I suppose, must have their privacy and their histories. It does not signify, as you say. Well, I had better release you to Mrs Poulter.'

Jenny hurried away, and Catherine was left to ponder the wisdom of listening to a chattering servant. Henry had not chosen to share with her that he had once been attached to a lady, and she supposed, in the greater schemes of God and man, it did not signify. She put away the questions which begged to be satisfied and reassured herself that soon enough an opportunity would arise in conversation and she might be able to ask him about it.

Even after her morning visit, without Henry the time seemed to drag on. It was only just gone one o' clock, so she ordered some tea and cake and spent an hour reading in her history book. Restless, and Henry's secret still on her mind, she left the house finally to walk amongst the myriad gardens in which the General took such pride. Unused to the contrived, orderly impression they gave off, her own home being as rambling and disorderly in style as this one was not, she found little in them to appeal to her taste. But she found it oddly interesting to watch three young men from the village toil away, digging, planting and watering, and when she came to the Pinery, the hothouse which was home to a dozen pineapple plants, she was interested enough to see where the exotic fruit on her plate in the evening came from. She had seen a pinery before, at Northanger, which was much larger, but that the General liked to have a hand in the estate at Woodston was clear enough, for the glass houses and gardens were much the same layout, even if smaller in number than those at Northanger.

After another long hour spent observing this industry, she found herself restless and low-spirited. Exhausted from doing nothing, when there was nothing to interest her or amuse her without Henry's being home, she wandered listlessly from room to room, expecting nothing and finding no disappointment in such expectations.

Wandering in due course down the back passage of the house again, past the door which had been forbidden her, she stopped before it. Idly, she pushed the wooden surface, expecting it to repel her hand with the same force as when she last tried it, but instead she gave a little gasp as it creaked and with a click, it swung open half an inch.

It was too much for Catherine, who was suffering from a dullness of spirits and want of company. Here was an adventure, a harmless one to her mind, for all she wanted was to see her own cellars and understand the rooms she might find below. She was much too sensible now to expect skeletons or any dreadful horrors, and it was highly unlikely that Mrs Poulter was concealing anything sinister below, but surely she must be allowed to explore her own house!

But she did not have a candle! She would see nothing without light. Disappointed, she closed the door again, careful so as not to close it fully, and sighed. She would have to wait for night-time when she could save her candle-stub and come down after everyone was in bed. Fortunately, Mrs Poulter had gone to the village for her afternoon off and was not due back until late evening. Perhaps the open door would go unnoticed by the servants. She could not bear it if she missed her one opportunity to explore below!

When Henry finally came home at half past four, it was to find Cathy sitting at the pianoforte determinedly playing her scales.

'I thought you had given up music,' quipped Henry when he looked around the door. 'What is it you feel so guilty about that you are to be found practising so diligently?'

Since it was just such a guilt which had promoted the sudden desire to self-flagellate at the pianoforte, she coloured at once and stammered, 'W-What can you mean but to make me nervous! Why, I managed that last scale very well until you came into the room!' She was crosser than she had meant to be and when her husband raised his eyebrows, she amended, 'I didn't mean I am not glad to see you, for I am — very much! How did you get on with your Mr Stevens?'

The distraction was enough to tempt Henry into a discussion of his curate and the distribution of tithes from last Sunday, and the rest of the day passed tolerably in talking and in dressing for dinner. If at her evening meal Catherine was a little quieter than usual, Henry did not appear to notice anything amiss, and by the time he was snoring comfortably in bed much later that evening, she had slipped from under the warm bedclothes, wrapped a shawl about her shoulders, and crept to the door. She waited for the candles to be snuffed out by Mrs Poulter, and once the woman's footsteps could no longer be heard on the landing, a deathly silence descended into the upper and lower realms of the house. Catherine crept from the room, holding a sputtering tallow candle. Finding the hallway quiet, she descended the stairs into the ground floor hall.

The forbidden door was as she had left it, not quite snibbed shut, and congratulating herself on her excellent luck, she repressed a youthful excitement and fortified herself for the adventure she had been privately wanting since Henry had become so absent at home. If anyone had reminded Catherine that idle hands make mischief, she might even have agreed, for in giving all the housekeeping up to Mrs Poulter, she had become as idle a young wife was ever to be found, and now that Henry had been from home so frequently, there was nothing but mischief to be made in the absence of occupation; she had nothing left to do in the world but find drama and adventure where industry and domestic cares might have kept her from harm. But none of these thoughts crossed Catherine's mind as she stood before the forbidden door.

Looking about her for the formidable Mrs Poulter, she was relieved to see no one lurking in the shadows, and she pushed open the door until she could see the stairwell descending before her. It looked surprisingly solid, not at all rickety as Mrs Poulter had given her to believe, and with a growing confidence, she stepped down onto the first wooden stair. She felt her way in the dim light. The banister was firm and after a dozen or so steps, she felt solid stone beneath her slippered feet and looked around her.

She found herself in a wine cellar of as modest proportions as befits a parsonage. Catherine, who had never seen Henry in his cups and did not imagine she would ever be confronted with such a circumstance, was therefore not at all surprised to note the smallness of the cellar lit up by her candle. Three walls of shelves on three sides of the room were built with wooden shelving, upon these being a haphazard collection of wine and port bottles, some crusty and dust-laden. A musty smell of old port wine assailed her nostrils. Stepping forward into the coolness of the cellar, emboldened by the comforting light of her candle, she examined the bottles briefly, slightly disappointed that there was nothing but what Mrs Poulter had already mentioned; no Japan stood against the wall, beckoning to be opened, no tall mysterious cupboard squatted hidden in the corner. And just as well she chided herself, for she would not dare to pry into them anyway! She had learned her lesson last year at Northanger!

Just as she had made up her mind to go back upstairs before she was missed, her eye came to rest on a dark shadow on the fourth wall, and moving nearer to it her heart skipped a beat. A doorway, which she had not noticed before, beckoned darkly. As if she could not compel her own feet, she stood for some time staring at the doorway, frozen in place.

'How silly,' she said out loud to herself. 'It is only a door to another room, in which I will find more bottles of wine, that is all!'

Moving closer with her sputtering light, she peered into the dark doorway, her breath held in a fright of anticipation. Catherine would have denied any hint that she had been expecting anything horrible; indeed, she was, she was quite convinced, cured of an overactive imagination and had no idea of submitting to idle fancy. But the very ordinary sight which the candle illuminated made her sigh all the same. No skeletons, no blood, and no mysterious papers with hieroglyphics were to be seen. Nor did any phantoms approach her in the darkness. All that met her curious eye was yet another wall lined with a few dusty bottles, and beside that an old cupboard, and on the floor sat a small chest.

Abandoning all her caution, so unconsciously ready to be shocked as she was, she was quite determined as she took her candle to the cupboard at once and ventured to open it. It was empty, and she closed the doors again with another little sigh. The chest, however, looked more inviting. It was not, she was relieved to find, Japan wood, but only ordinary chestnut or something of the kind.

Observing with great disappointment that there was no key for the lock, she was about to turn away when she noticed upon the opposite shelf, next to a gardening fork, there lay a small silver key. Curiously, it was not dusty, but gleamed as if it had been recently used. Placing her candle tremulously upon the shelf, she took the key up, her cheeks flushed, and bent to try it in the lock. It was too dark to see her own hand, and making a little noise of frustration, she seized up her candle and held it close. She turned the key. The lock gave way smoothly and Catherine, who always thought afterward that she should have remembered there and then Henry's advice about curiosity and hell being close companions, lifted the lid of the chest, and gasped.

What met her eye at the first moments of their gazing upon the contents caused her to stop and stare. It was not as if she had expected a skeleton, or anything such thing — indeed she was much too cured of romantic imaginings to expect anything so grim. But the sight of a gold ring, inset with a lock of fair hair, and a cream lace handkerchief, sitting on the bottom of the chest, astonished her all the same.

'How odd!' she pronounced to herself. Without thinking, she reached for the handkerchief, and brought it up to the candlelight to inspect. In one corner, the initials "E.P" were monogrammed in blue thread. But who could have left their pretty kerchief in a chest in the wine cellar? Who was "E.P"? And whose ring was it, and whose hair was set into it? Did Mrs Poulter after all have a secret to conceal in the cellar? And why would she hide such innocuous items?

Catherine, wishing for diversion, hoping for mystery, and expecting nothing of either sort, could not say that she was disappointed. She had not been foolish enough, she told herself, to expect skeletons nor any dreadful sights, but this — this was at least a mystery to occupy her mind harmlessly.

Closing the chest, the items now replaced as they had been found, she took her now fast-dimming candle and retreated upstairs, taking care to make no sound as she closed the door to the cellar.

"She lifted the lid of the chest
and gasped."

In their chamber, Henry had not stirred. Catherine crept quietly beneath the soft covers and allowed the warmth to seep back into her limbs. Her mind was for some time occupied with reflections upon the evening's activities, and it was well after the clock had struck two before she finally closed her eyes.

Six

Numerous questions occupied Catherine's mind for the next two days, but she could speculate no satisfactory answer. Of course, it had occurred to her almost immediately to tell Henry of her find in the cellar, but besides her guilt on account of going into the forbidden cellar in the first place, there was also the other troubling fact to consider; it was clearly Mrs Poulter who had left the objects there, and despite her dislike for the woman, she would not like to cause trouble between the servant and Henry. After some consideration, she determined finally to wait until she could discover the answer to the mystery for herself.

A few days after Catherine's odd discovery in the wine cellar, a letter came for Henry, by urgent delivery, and which seemed to put him into an unusual ill humour. Not used to finding her cheerful Henry in a disagreeable mood, Catherine was anxious. He had retired to his study after opening the letter, and he remained there the rest of the day. He had refused tea, too, and been short with Jenny.

When he appeared in the dining room that evening, his countenance was solemn, and Catherine could hardly raise a smile from him. She noted he had barely touched his soup, or his wine.

After an almost silent first course, and the gammon ham and boiled fish had both been served, she had sent the servant from the room. As soon as the door had closed on them, she had tentatively spoken. 'I hate to see you so out of sorts, my love. Was it the letter you received?'

Henry did not immediately reply, but put down his knife. 'I am sorry, my dear, if I have been a little out of sorts.'

'Was it *very* bad news? Or — I hope I have not done anything to displease you?'

He met her gaze with attempted cheerfulness. 'No, indeed, it is nothing of any importance. I only have a most plaguing headache, but a good night's sleep will cure me, I am sure.' He gave her a reassuring smile.

'Oh! But I am very sorry for you, indeed! A headache! They are the most unpleasant things to bear! Would you like to me to give you my lavender water? Or take a little tea? I will have Jenny bring willow bark; perhaps it will help. Mrs Allen swears by it for herself, you know.'

Henry declined lavender, accepted the offer of tea, and by the time the clock intoned nine hours, he was restored almost to his old self, consented to play at cribbage, and urged Catherine to play two or three tunes which she had been working on, although they were simple and she soon tired of playing them.

'I daresay you think me shockingly unmusical, for you have always heard Eleanor's playing, which is very fine and everything it ought to be for one so inclined to the instrument; but if its only you who shall hear me, I can hardly scruple to decline on account of it!' she lamented after she had finished the third piece. 'I am surprised you can still love me after hearing me play.'

'If I could not separate you and your playing, then I would be a very unfortunate man,' replied Henry, much amused. 'But as I love you as well now as I did two months ago, you are safe from danger.'

Catherine waited for Jane to take away the tea things, and once she had quitted the room, went to Henry, sat herself upon his knee and kissed him sweetly. 'I am glad you are feeling more yourself. I was quite alarmed. I cannot bear to think you angry with me — I suppose it was that horrid letter which put you all in a bad humour?'

'Is there anything for me to be angry about?'

'No, nothing! Will you tell me what was in your letter? Was it bad news?'

Henry shook his head. 'I confess I was not happy to receive the news contained in the letter, but more I cannot tell you, Catherine. Pray don't press the point. It is nothing for you to be anxious about.

But I must go away tomorrow, however sorry I am for it.'

Catherine's face, always open, and her feelings plain, wore a look of dismay.'Go away?' she cried, 'but for how long? Must you really?'

'Aye,' replied Henry, 'I must. I have business in town which I must attend to, although it gives me no pleasure, I am sure, to leave you, nor to spend three days away from Woodston. But, I hope that knowing I intend to bring you a present on my return may do a little to soften the blow of being separated from me for a few days.'

Catherine was now all curiosity to know more of her promised present, but Henry would not budge. 'Nay,' said he, 'if I was to spoil the surprise, then you would have no reason to pine for my return. I must have you red-eyed, and longing for my return, and weeping into your diary at night, or how shall I ever know if you truly love me or not?'

'Stop teasing me this instant, Henry Tilney! You know very well what my feelings are. Very well, go away, if you must, only can you not give me just a little hint of what your object is in going to town?'

'None at all,' replied Henry cheerfully.

'But I recall your telling me last week that Captain Tilney is presently in town! Of course — you are going to congratulate your brother on his engagement!'

Henry had received a letter from his father the previous week which had announced Fredrick Tilney's recent engagement to a Miss Sweeting of Bath, heir to an independent fortune of as many thousand as must be considered a great addition to the comparatively meagre fortunes of an army captain, who with all his merits, could be master of only a few hundred pounds. Frederick Tilney would, someday, inherit Northanger Abbey, and the income it commanded, but seeing as the upkeep of the Abbey was barely equal to its income, the General had set his hopes upon his oldest son to marry well in order to supply the difference wanted.

Therefore, Frederick's announcement had been a cause for celebration, not least for General Tilney, who having been made tolerably content on the marriage of his daughter to nobility, now had the joy of knowing his oldest son was to marry a fortune. It was, he had written, a triumph to be reckoned as only what was rightfully due his oldest son.

The General had long been discovered by Catherine to be more interested in money than in the comfort or happiness of his sons and daughter, so it was no shock to her that the General had had more to say in his letter on the pecuniary advantages to the Tilney family of this alliance, than of the personal happiness his son might derive from such a union. But Henry, who had benefitted materially from his sister's marriage by the hastening of his only wish — to marry Catherine — had little enough stake in this second announcement to be much more than merely complaisant on the topic. However, he had enough Christian sentiment in him to be as happy for his brother as he could be when they had never been particularly intimate.

He said now, 'Naturally, I shall congratulate Frederick in person while I am there.'

'How strange to imagine Captain Tilney in love!' declared Catherine. 'He always seemed quite — quite — reserved in that regard. He did not seem to be ready to fall in love.' She blushed, for she would not speak ill of Henry's brother.

Henry understood her meaning, however. 'You are thinking of Miss Thorpe, I suppose, and the unfortunate business at Bath last year. Your friend was cruelly used, yes, but I know you do not forget the mischief which can be done by an unprincipled girl. Your brother James was the greatest sufferer, and Miss Thorpe readily admitted my brother's attentions, as much as *he* was following the unprincipled male instinct.'

Catherine blushed again; she was now a married lady and knew first-hand of the male instinct. 'Isabella did my brother a great injustice, indeed! But Henry, you do not mean that your brother was justified in his actions simply because he is a man and unable to rule his — his instincts?'

Henry was amused. 'My dear Kitty, I see that I am to be wary with you, and to have more thought before I speak, for you discover too much meaning in my words; indeed, I had no such notion, excepting that my brother has no extraordinary regard for the things that others would find a restraint on their behaviours. I only meant that if a man exploits a female such as your friend Miss Thorpe, it is to my own mind, of less a consequence than if he had preyed upon an innocent, untainted, unworldly female.'

To this Catherine could hardly agree, there being a differing principle upon which she had been brought up, but her own filial loyalty was so strong that she was unable to find anything disagreeable in Henry for his own, and so she resolved to keep her doubts to herself. Instead, she ventured to ask, 'Then do you think Captain Tilney so incapable of altering his character, or coming to regret his ways, that he may not behave in a just and kind way to any female? Perhaps he really has changed!'

Henry raised his brows and said warmly, 'You feel, as always, what is the greatest credit to human nature. As I have said before, Cathy, you are superior in good nature to the rest of the world. I am an old cynic, and what I have done to deserve you I can hardly imagine! Perhaps some alteration of character is possible with anyone, given the right motivations. Although I can hardly account for Frederick's wishing to give up single life and the freedoms which come with it. But if he is to inherit Northanger, then I suppose he must have something to live upon. The income from the old place is hardly fit to sustain a young man as lively as my brother.'

'So you think your brother cannot be in love, then?' replied Catherine doubtfully. 'But surely he cannot want for money, for he is not poor, is he?'

'Perhaps he *has* fallen prey to cupid's arrow, but I find it difficult to believe. He is by no means living with out-turned pockets — my father supplements his income quite generously, I believe — but Frederick has always had expensive tastes — and expensive hobbies,' replied Henry dryly.

'So you *do* think his object is to marry for money? My mother and father always taught me that it was excessively evil indeed, to do such a thing!'

Henry smiled. 'And so it is, when one loving heart is duped into joining with another mercenary one. But in most cases, such a union is to the mutual satisfaction of both parties. My brother and I, as you know Catherine, live our lives very differently to each other. I am happy for him, and glad that he has decided at last to settle down. As for his motive, he must live with his choices. But I confess I am all curiosity to meet this young woman who will need a great deal of fortitude and spirit to consider a life with my brother!'

'Why do you so dislike Captain Tilney?' asked Catherine tentatively. 'I have a good reason to dislike him just a little — his stealing Isabella away last year when were all in Bath together, while she was engaged to my brother — I still cannot forget it, but you — he has done nothing to *you*, has he?'

Henry sighed. 'Not to me personally. And yet, I confess I am uneasy. Frederick is — shall we say — a lively young man. I would not go so far as to call him dissolute, but he has his vices. My father is too lenient with him, and even Eleanor — but it is not my place to say more. I cannot speak ill of Frederick for he is still my brother and heir to Northanger. No, I can see you are a curious creature, my dear, but curiosity is the companion to mischief, as they say. Do not press me anymore.'

The idea that Henry had secrets from her would, not very long ago, have been a strange notion to Catherine, but now she was inured to the idea, having already become aware of at least one part of Henry's history which had been kept from her. Besides that, she allowed that any young man and his brother might share a few jealousies or disagreements. Captain Tilney was, from her own estimation, if not a dissolute young man, then a heartless one, and after Isabella was enticed by him to give up the engagement to her brother James the previous year, she could not form a better opinion of him just yet. But he was now her brother-in-law, and she was generous enough to allow for changes of heart. Perhaps the love a good woman night work wonders upon the character of a wilful young man who had been given the reins of his own life too much, and had no steady example in his father to curb his appetite for pleasure-seeking.

Seven

Henry's three day's absence was a daunting prospect to Catherine, for two reasons. Part of her dismay was testimony to the tender esteem in which she held her husband, but if she were to confess it, the prospect of spending three days at home with Mrs Poulter always to be coming upon her suddenly did nothing to calm, and everything to agitate, her nerves. Usually when Henry was away from home for the day, which was more and more often, she hid herself in her own little sitting-room, or she went out to walk or ride, but the weather was now growing colder and she looked upon three days inside shut up with only the servants and Mrs Poulter with a great deal of gloomy anticipation. She said as much to Henry as they prepared for bed.

Henry had been almost amused, however, at her nervousness to be alone at the parsonage with Mrs Poulter. 'This present circumstance affords every occasion you have been wishing for, Kitty, to learn the workings of Woodston parsonage if you would but seize it; I would be excessively pleased, my love, if you could try to put away your timidness with Mrs P and learn to be confident as the mistress of Woodston.'

With these words, kindly given but firmly meant, Catherine was shamed, and at once determined to spend Henry's absence improving her housekeeping skills. With this object in mind, she was up at dawn the following day to see Henry away, and then proceeded down to the hen house with the object of collecting the eggs and feeding the pigs, before Jenny herself came out.

Timidly investigating the barn, she saw that it was much like the barn at home, and the grain barrel quite the same as was used at her father's house. She took up a large scoop of the wheat which was stored in the barrel in the corner, and she made her way out to the henhouse. Opening the door to the pen, a multitude of eleven hens rushed to her, and made as if to peck her feet. Squealing, she reeled back in fright and a large quantity of the wheat spilled from the china bowl over the courtyard. The hens, seeing their unexpected advantage and determined not to lose a minute in seizing it, celebrated their new-found freedom by running out the open door and immediately scattered over the cobbled courtyard to furiously peck at the delicious grain, while Catherine clapped a hand to her mouth. As she tried to shoo them away inside the henhouse again, they eyed her with beady-eyed contrariness and quickly ran in every direction but the one she wished them to go.

'Good heavens! Come back here at once!' she commanded them breathlessly, dashing at the nearest ones.

They studiously ignored her and begun to run in zigzags in front of her. As soon as she had one creature squawking and flapping furiously in her arms, the others would dash just as nimbly in the opposite direction, cackling as they did so.

'Mrs Tilney! Whatever are you doing, Ma'am?'

Catherine spun around, an offended hen in her arms, her cheeks crimson. Jenny stood at the kitchen door, viewing the scene with astonishment.

'I was only feeding the hens — I mean, I never meant to let them out, but I spilled the wheat and suddenly they were everywhere and —'

Already the dog had begun to chase one of the hens, barking excitedly, while Jenny had begun to run toward the barn herself. 'Why ever are you feeding the hens, at all, and what is this wheat doing all about on the ground? It is corn we feed the hens, Ma'am, if you please. Never mind that hen, but do go and shut the gate before they see it is open!'

Just as Catherine was about to run to the gate, Mrs Poulter strode past and shut the little gate into the kitchen garden herself. But before Catherine could stammer her apologies, the hen being chased by the dog had taken urgent flight over the fence and disappeared into the field beyond. Red-faced, Catherine turned to Mrs Poulter in contrition. 'I am very sorry indeed, I only—'

" 'Good heavens! Come back here,'
she commanded them
breathlessly."

'Mrs Tilney! Do go inside, if you don't mind, and let Jenny gather the hens into the pen — those which are left, that is,' the housekeeper added coldly. 'If you wish to feed the hens in future, ask one of the servants to show you how, if you please.'

Catherine, humiliated beyond what she could bear, and at her own hand, could barely reply, but took herself into the house and ran upstairs to her room, there to cast herself on her bed. The indignity of being ordered from her own courtyard was exceeded only by the mortification of having her humiliation come at the hand of Mrs Poulter, the very person whom she wished to think well of her. It was a great suffering Catherine was forced to endure for the next hour, being too frightened to go downstairs, and it was midday before she ventured, red-eyed and pale, to leave her room. She spent the rest of the afternoon in the drawing room, cast into a melancholy, until Emily came with a tray of fresh tea and plum cake to soothe her spirits.

~ ~ * ~ ~

It had not been an auspicious start. Nothing she did seemed to go well, and for the first time, Catherine really did take herself to task for her lack of attention in her younger years, to the instruction of her long-suffering mama. She searched her mind and found it wanting in all the practical skills which should have come easily to the daughter of a clergyman, raised in a parsonage just like this, and with no excuse in the world not to have shown some interest in hen-keeping, swine-herding, cheese making, and milking. Betsy the cow, thought Catherine ruefully, knew more of the business of cheese and butter making than did Catherine herself.

But self-delusion and stubborn inattentiveness must be wanting only genuine desire to improve to make them yield something half-pleasing, and Catherine had enough of the last to find herself desiring very much to do better. By the same time the next day, Catherine, a young lady who had no natural talent for introspection and self-knowledge, had come to the beginning of an understanding of just how she much she lacked of the practical skills required for life as a parson's wife. Recalling Henry's fortifying words before he had left, she determined anew to make those additions to her knowledge which would make him proud of her. How silly she had been to think that to be able to play a tune creditably, or to paint a picture wherein all the foremost objects were at least recognisable as themselves, were all the improvements she had needed to make. She was humble enough to admit she had been complaisant in allowing Mrs Poulter to make all the decisions, and she to accept them all without making an attempt to understand them. When Henry came home, such a change he would see, she was determined.

And she would begin with something a little less able to go awry than chickens. Perhaps she would simply make a beginning by asking Jenny about washing day. She might even help! The nature of her next task decided upon, she began immediately by seeking out Jenny and asking if she might watch her do the wash, so as to learn. Jenny, however, was doubtful.

'Why would you want to know how to do the wash, Ma'am, when you will never need to wash your own bloomers, let alone your own gowns?' she chattered as she counted away the plate from breakfast. 'And I don't know as what Mrs P would say, if she were to find out you'd been lurking about down here with the servants. Perhaps you'd be best as staying above stairs, if you know what I mean, Mrs Tilney. I can get Emily to explain the silver to you, if you want to feel like you are doing something, although Lord knows why you'd not be at your pianoforte or your easel like most other young ladies.'

'But I'm not another young lady!' cried Catherine in frustration. 'I am supposed to be a parson's wife and I hardly know how my own household runs. I must learn something sensible. I confess I have neglected my education, but it is never too late, surely!'

'Well,' replied Jenny thoughtfully, 'I suppose there can be no harm in you watching how the wash is done. Did you never see your own servants at home do the wash, Ma'am?'

'No, never — that is, I confess I had my head too much in books, to pay any attention to how Mama ran the house. But that is all over with now — I am determined to learn it all!'

For all her enthusiasm, after a half hour or so, Catherine thought to herself that doing wash was quite a tedious and tiring affair. Jenny showed her the huge copper and how they heated water for it, but once the clothes and bed linens had been put in to steam and the lye soap added, the endless scrubbing seemed to Catherine to be the most labouring and dull employments one could do. She tried her hand at scrubbing, but the water was too hot for her skin, and the lye burned, and she soon gave it up. 'I don't know how you do it, Jenny,' said she, drying her hands. 'I think I shall always feel guilty now, when I send my things downstairs to be washed, knowing how long it takes just to boil the water and scrub a petticoat!'

Jenny was cheerful. 'Aye, Ma'am, but it must be done, for who else is there?'

Who else indeed, thought Catherine as Jenny left her to fetch more hot water. Looking around the scullery room she spied Henry's silk cravats, which while he was away, he had given to his man to see laundered. She took them up in her hand. These were small, and not, surely, too difficult to clean. She could easily scrub these in the hot water, and once they were clean she could show them to Henry and he would see how she was trying very hard to become a better wife to him!

Pleased with her notion, she dropped them into the hot water, and began to gently scrub them with the little switch of horse hair which Jenny had used on the calico petticoat. A few minutes later she was pleased with her endeavours, and as Jenny was just coming back with another kettle of hot water, she held them up. 'Look, I have managed to clean Mr Tilney's cravats! Do not you think I have made a good job of it?'

Jenny stood still and paled. 'Lor! Mrs Tilney, what have you done! Them cravats is going to be no good to the master now! What in the world was you thinking of, putting them in the hot water!'

Catherine blanched and let Jenny take the delicate, steaming items from her hand. 'What do you mean? What in the world is wrong?'

'Oh dear! I am sorry to say it Ma'am, but hot water injures silk. These cravats, I'm afraid, will shrink vastly, and be no more use to poor Mr Tilney.'

Catherine could hardly speak. She stood, her cheeks as crimson as her now reddened hands, and tried not to cry. 'I didn't know about the hot water and the silk. I — Mama never told me — or I suppose I didn't heed her,' she added miserably. 'Can they be pulled into shape, or— or— perhaps I could buy him new ones...'

Jenny sighed and patted her arm. 'Now, Mrs Tilney, never mind it, it weren't your fault you didn't know about washing silk, although you might have waited until I came back before you tried to clean them. But Mr Tilney loves you so much that it will hardly signify, I am sure.'

Catherine, now caught up in misery, left the offending scraps of boiled cloth and went in a great misery upstairs to her room. She felt that all her attempts to make a housekeeper of herself, and a better wife to Henry, were to no avail. She was quite useless, and it was her own fault for not paying more heed to her mama.

Feeling unutterably miserable and wholly cast down, she left her room and went to sit in the garden, on the swinging love-seat under the willow tree, hoping to keep out of Mrs Poulter's way. Hidden behind the hedge and shaded by the long-armed, half-bare branches of the tree, it was not long before she allowed herself, in privacy, to give way to a few tears, and then for tears to turn to sobs. Henry must surely despise her. Surely she must now lose his entire regard! 'Oh,' cried she into her muslin skirts, 'He will scold me so dreadfully and see me for the foolish girl he has married!'

'If you mean your husband, I am sure you cannot have done anything dreadful enough for him to scold you so severely.'

Mr Longstaff's chocolate tones intruded on her privacy and Catherine started up, scrambling off the seat and wiping her cheeks with her palms. He had just come around the hedge on his way to the house and stood not three yards from her.

'Goodness me! Mr Longstaff! — of course! I quite forgot! It is Tuesday! I shall go inside and collect up my drawing things —' Her cheeks were pink with embarrassment.

Longstaff eyed her for a moment, then reaching into his pocket, held out a kerchief.

After a moment, she accepted the linen square, and wiped her eyes with it. 'Thank you. You are very kind.'

'I am at your service, Mrs Tilney.' He paused a moment, then said in tones much softened, 'I am sorry to see you so indisposed. Perhaps I might be able to assist?' He indicated the garden bench from which she had just gotten up.

Catherine, too in need of comfort at that moment to hesitate long, allowed the gallant Mr Longstaff to hand her back to her place on the bench. He waited until she was settled, then politely seated himself beside her.

It did not take much urging to provoke a confession. Catherine related the unfortunate tale of the silk cravats and her efforts to improve her house-keeping skills. 'And so you see, I have only made everything worse, and goodness knows what Mrs Poulter thinks of me, and Henry will come home and find his cravats ruined, and I will lose his good favour — if I had it at all, for I have proven to be very foolish and sad wife thus far! I know it is my own doing, but it doesn't make it any more bearable, you know!'

'But do you suppose your husband to be so very formidable? I have never thought him an ogre, you know. Although I am only tolerably acquainted with your husband, he always appeared to me as a sensible man, not prone to fits of anger.'

'No indeed, not anger!' she said very earnestly. 'He is always very kind to me. But Mrs Poulter will most certainly tell him what I did with the chickens, and even if Jenny does not mention the mishap with the cravats, Henry will surely miss them within a day!'

A fresh tear slid its way down a flushed and pretty cheek, and Longstaff slid a little closer. 'I see your predicament, Mrs Tilney. But it is a great shame to cry and make those pretty blue eyes red and puffy.'

'You are very kind, but I cannot help but think I am a great goose and that Henry will think so too, when he hears of what I have done. And I didn't even tell you about the chickens!'

Longstaff smiled and patted her hand comfortingly. 'Chickens! Ah, well, never mind about that. I rather think you have had a very eventful few days, and all on your own, too! Now, I will tell you something.' His voice was low and velvety. 'You have done very well, in my own opinion, to manage things alone in the absence of your husband — it is more than my own sisters would have attempted, I can tell you! Pray do not shake that pretty head! It is true. You did not give in to indolence and dullness, but sought to improve yourself; you did not wait for others to take the lead, but made an exemplary start by showing yourself willing. You have given the servants an example from which to learn. Yes, you may look at me in astonishment, but it is all quite true. You are not as hopeless a case as you believe, Mrs Tilney.'

'Do you really think so?' she replied doubtfully, a little disconcerted to be called pretty with such sincerity. 'I only hope that my husband can think of my silly scrapes the same way!'

'Perhaps,' came that gentleman's rejoinder smoothly, 'he should have known better than to leave you alone, after you have been so soon married? But then, I am sure it would only be the most pressing and urgent business to take him away from so lovely a young lady as yourself.'

He was smiling at her. A charming, disconcerting smile.

She shook herself. 'Oh! Oh no, it is not like *that!* At least, Henry does not go away *very* much — unless it is urgent. That is, he is often away, but there is a lot to do, and he never leaves me alone for more than a day. Apart from this time, I mean.' A brief interval of awkward silence passed and she broke her gaze to look away up at the house windows. A curtain twitched at one of the upper room windows, and Catherine, conscious of how it must look to be sitting so close to a gentleman not her husband in the privacy of the garden, self-consciously stood up. 'Perhaps — I am a little tired, Mr Longstaff. Do you think I might postpone our lesson until my husband returns? I think I am too anxious to heed anything just now!'

'Of course.' Longstaff, eyeing the same window, stood also, bowed, and picked up his hat which he had placed at his side. 'I shall call in a few days. Good morning!'

Eight

A three day's absence, fraught with scrapes and mishaps, and the cool regard of Mrs Poulter whenever she came into company with the woman, was enough to have poor Catherine unsure if she dreaded or welcomed the return of her husband. I shall not say she wept herself to sleep each night, but if her pillow was a little damp in the mornings, it was not remarked upon by Emily, who came to draw the curtains and pour fresh water into the ewer. The third day Catherine expected Henry home every hour from the time she rose. But her wait was not long, and by and by Henry' horse was seen on the drive, and after a short delay of a fifteen minutes in which every minute saw Catherine become more and more anxious, he finally made his appearance in the drawing room. Catherine, full of dread mingled with delight to have him home again, went to him for a kiss, then led him to the chaise in front of the fire.

To her anxious state, his greeting to her seemed a little cool, but presently, after calling for Emily to bring some spruce beer and bread and cheese, he sighed and walked over to the window.

'And how was your journey?' Catherine asked anxiously. 'Did you happen to see Captain Tilney in town?'

'I did see my brother, but not in town, for he was at Northanger when I called in on my way up to London.'

'Oh! So you have seen your father and brother, then? I hope you found them in good health – I suppose Captain Tilney talked much of his marriage?'

'Not so very much, as it happened, for he left almost as soon as I arrived.' Henry frowned a little. 'Do you recollect that I promised you a present, before I went away?'

'Yes! Only I don't think I deserve any presents,' she added sadly. 'It is very kind but —'

'I did not bring anything back, so it cannot signify now. Pray don't look so alarmed, my little Kitty, for it is nothing to do with you. Let me tell you what has happened. My mother left each of her children some jewellery, very good pieces which had been in her family for some time. Eleanor was given hers when our mother died, but Frederick and I were expected to keep ours for the occasion of our marriages, as gifts for our betrothed. It was my portion which I purposed to give to you, and for which reason I stopped overnight at Northanger, to ask for it. Only, upon my going to her room to collect it, I found that it was gone, and Frederick's pieces too.'

Catherine's countenance was dismay and astonishment. 'Do you think your father might have moved them? Or perhaps they had been put in another room?'

Henry shook his head. 'I am afraid my father had no knowledge of their being gone, and a search of the house was carried out to no avail. I am afraid, Catherine, that two rather valuable pieces I wished you to have cannot go to their rightful owner. I am very sad for it, but there is nothing to be done at present.'

His countenance showed all his regret, and Catherine was at once melted. Never inclined to missishness, and not taught to expect pretty baubles, her only concern must be for Henry. 'Never mind that,' she cried warmly, 'for myself I never expected a present so great, and therefore it can be of no consequence to *me* not to receive such a gift, but I must feel everything proper for *you*, at the loss of your mother's jewellery, perhaps the only reminder you have of her affection. I am excessively sorry for you indeed!'

Henry looked his gratitude for her warm concern and told her so. 'Still, it pains me that I had promised, and now I have nothing to give. My father has sworn to look into the matter, to interrogate every servant. He is much disturbed — indeed, he is excessively angry on account of their being my mother's things and owed to us, his children. He will get to the bottom of the theft, but for now, you must resolve to fortify yourself to going to church without such finery. Perhaps fine jewellery such as you deserve will surely follow, if I can but discover where it is gone and who has taken it!'

'But you know I care little for finery! I mean, it is all very nice, but I hardly rely — oh, you tease me again! But Henry, was not your brother very bitter, to know he cannot give his own wife her part of his mother's legacy?'

'I doubt Frederick has ever been accused of wearing his emotions on his sleeve,' remarked Henry dryly, 'but even so, I perceived in his countenance a certain uneasiness and disappointment. I am sure he feels as much as he ought in the circumstance, but we must consider that his future bride comes from a wealthy family; it can be of little consequence to *her* if her husband cannot make her a present of a few jewels, although the pieces set aside for Frederick were valuable enough. Still, it is the pride of a man which is most injured when he cannot bring *something* to a marriage, especially if it is a materially unequal one. I confess I did feel for him although his circumstance is not quite the same as our own.'

'It is a very shocking business, altogether,' replied Catherine. 'I cannot help but feel wounded for you both, and for the General too. It would be quite dreadful if the thief were some staff, or a close friend of the family! I suppose it could not be anyone else, as no one else would know where to look — your mother's rooms are kept quite under lock and key by the General, are not they?'

Henry conceded, then said, 'And yet, there is nothing to be gained by surmising, so for now let us talk of pleasanter matters.'

Emily now came in with spruce beer and a tray of refreshments. When she had quitted the room, and Henry had helped himself, Catherine asked tentatively, 'Did you complete your business in town?'

'I did.'

'Then Henry, I hope you have come home a happier man than when you left Woodston three days ago; then you were all distraction and ill-humour. I did not like it at all!'

Henry looked his remorse. 'And so I was, but all that is at an end now. My business has been almost concluded, and I cannot say more. But you have not told me yet how you amused yourself while I was gone away.'

Catherine, who could not want a more open invitation to confess her tale of woe, and could not think of hiding anything from Henry, began at once to relate her misadventures with the hens and the cravats. When she had finished, she could not tell what Henry was thinking. It looked very much as if he was trying excessively hard to repress a smile.

He began with mock sternness. 'Really Catherine! If this is how you mean to carry on then you must give everything over to Mrs Poulter, for we cannot have any more hens lost, and as for the cravats, I am in agony, for you know I count my cravats as among my most valued acquaintances.'

'Do stop teasing me, Henry. I know very well you mean to torment my feelings and it is quite cruel of you! I have been in a great anxiety about it for these two days past! Are you seriously very angry with me? I have been quite excessively anxious since it happened!'

'My little pea-goose! Perhaps I am a *little* cross about the cravats, but it hardly signifies as my parish will not notice, I will venture to say, the difference between my best silk cravats and my second-best ones. As for the hen, I am sure she will come home in a day or two, and if she does not, you must forgo your egg at breakfast, and that is as serious a punishment as I can contemplate.'

Catherine was, however, determined to contend with comfort and resisted its approaches. She was still mortified. 'I only wanted to learn, and show you that I am not such a scatterbrain after all, and I did not mean to let out the hens, only they are so quick! I couldn't bear it if you were angry with me, Henry! Even if I deserve it very much!'

Laughing, Henry patted his knee. 'Come here my little Kitty. That's better, is it not?' He positioned her on his lap and put his arms around her. 'I cannot sanction the results of your rather hair-brained schemes in my absence, but I can approbate the motives which drive them. Now give me a kiss and tell me you are very sorry, and we will forget such things ever happened.'

Catherine, full of relief, did as she was bid, and inwardly rejoiced that she had married such a mild-tempered and devoted husband.

That evening, Henry was particularly kind and attentive to her, and in the course of the evening, by means of a lively game of cribbage, her spirits were once more raised to a tolerable composure. But, when she was in bed later that night, listening to Henry's quiet breathing, she could not but help recall what Mr Longstaff had said about Henry's leaving her alone being a little unfair. She was not sure he was right on that account, but Henry had been absent more than she had expected him to be, and within her heart she was ashamed to find burning there a tiny flame of resentment that he would leave her alone to cope by herself so much. Nevertheless, she resolved, she would do better tomorrow, and such was the relief to feel herself out of danger, that she succumbed to sleep only seconds after such thoughts had passed through her mind.

Nine

It might seem, dear reader, that providence is often as fickle as it is unfair. Certainly it was not at all kind to Catherine, for a few days after Henry came home from his mysterious business in London, his curate was suddenly called away on account of a family illness, and Henry's duty was to his parish in the absence of his curate. Catherine endured Henry's ever-increasing absences with a cheerful spirit, and spent some of the time calling upon the sick and poor, but after a fort'night in which she saw him only infrequently, his being gone from the house before breakfast and arriving home sometimes too late for dinner, the little flame of resentment which had been burning in her bosom was fanned into a crackling fire which made her sometimes short with him, and more and more unhappy whenever he was gone.

At first she made excuses for Henry to herself, that he was busy, and the parish business took him from home more than he would like, but a little voice taunted her too, in moments of idle reflection, that perhaps she had displeased him so much that he needed to leave her company for longer periods. It was hard to forgive herself for the silly scrapes she had got herself into, and if Mrs Poulter had made clear her disdain for the sad lack of housekeeping skills so openly exhibited by the new mistress of Woodston, then surely Henry must be feeling such a circumstance even more so. Catherine so wanted his good opinion, that it almost pained her physically to think that she might have lost it.

She did her best to become a good parson's wife; her visits to the poor and sickly were regular, she arranged flowers for the little church, and she stood at her husband's side every Sunday after service, greeting and smiling. She continued to read in her history books, to paint and to draw, to embroider her screen neatly, and to sometimes make half-hearted attempts at her pianoforte. She tried once to darn her husband's stockings, but getting the thread in a tangle, and unable to copy what she had seen Jenny doing, she gave up the notion after only a few minutes.

When Henry was home for a whole day, which did not happen very often, he made a point of riding out with her, and on these occasions, it was so almost like the first month, when he was attentive and never from home, that she felt churlish and silly for feeling resentful at his absence. But these days did not happen often, and on the odd occasion that she did ride alone, she found more than once her melancholy was so strong that she was unable to prevent a tear or two running down her cheek.

Catherine was never melancholy for long, however, her spirits being fashioned by nature for cheerfulness, and for the most part she got on with forming herself into a more accomplished lady and a more useful wife. Nothing had been discovered of the location of the lost jewellery, and the topic had ceased to be canvassed between them at dinner. Catherine's thoughts were sometimes occupied with her mysterious discovery in the wine cellar however, and she even considered the possibility that somehow, Henry's early attachment may have something to do with the handkerchief and locket. The initials on the handkerchief were "E.P" and Jenny had clearly called the young lady "Miss Parkhurst." But why items belonging to a female who had never been at Woodston could be hidden in a cellar, Catherine could not imagine, and so she dismissed this idea almost as soon as she had thought of it.

She had once or twice considered asking Henry about the matter, but she did not wish to expose Jenny's thoughtless comments and risk her position, and besides, it was in the past, and Catherine felt that a young man must be allowed his secrets, so long as they remained in the past. It seemed, however, as if there were more secrets hidden at Woodston than she had ever cared to know or would ever solve. The mystery of the hidden handkerchief and ring, the secrets which Henry hid about the mysterious letter, his trip to London, and about his past *amour* which he had never thought pertinent to tell her about — all weighed upon her more heavily each day. And besides these, Mrs Poulter's disapproval of her and her own distressing attempts to learn to be a better wife seemed to doom her to failure.

If these secrets had not been enough in number, Catherine shortly added another to the now bulging reticule she carried about in her mind. She had once or twice spotted Mrs Poulter going down into the forbidden wine cellar and had assumed that the housekeeper was going to fetch up a bottle of port or wine for Henry, or for Cook to use. But on one occasion, she happened upon the woman just coming back up the cellar stairs and as the housekeeper had peeped into the dim hallway, she had seemed furtive, looking around her before she stepped out fully.

Catherine, who had been providentially concealed by dimness at the top of the stair above, was able to look down, unseen, and watch as the woman had almost crept from the cellar door, looked around, and quietly closed and locked the door after her, then carried on down the hall. It was not so much the secretive nature of her actions, however, that stuck Catherine, but the fact that she carried no bottle under her arm. Why would Mrs Poulter go into the cellar, and leave again, with no bottle? There was nothing else in the cellar, save the handkerchief and ring, which could draw her there. If Catherine had wanted a confirmation of Mrs Poulter's connection with the items at the bottom of the chest, this was it.

~ ~ * ~ ~

With Henry being so often from home, and loneliness creeping in upon her, Catherine had begun to take great comfort in being able to express herself with paper and paint. One afternoon, she had set up her painting things in the cool winter sun in the back garden. Here, Jenny and Emily were often going in and out to beat carpets and taking care of domestic duties. Today their presence felt cheerful to Catherine who had been starved for company of late. It was Tuesday and Mr Longstaff had come, begun her lesson, and left her briefly alone to practice the techniques she had just learned. Her subject was a watercolour scene with a lake and trees. It was a simple study, but in her present state of mind, she had painted it with rather more moodiness than she had intended.

After a time spent walking around the garden, observing the carpet-beating endeavours of the two servants, and stopping to talk to them briefly, Longstaff had approached Catherine and looked over her work. Catherine sighed deeply and dabbed and blurred her colours, trying to remember how he had taught her.

'Very pretty. A little gloomy, but altogether an improvement on your last.'

'You flatter my attempts on each occasion, Mr Longstaff. How shall I ever know if I have really improved, if I can never trust your word?' she laughed.

'Oh, that was not intended to flatter at all. I would never scruple to criticise, you know! No, you improve by degrees, under your own merits.'

'The degrees, Mr Longstaff, must be very small indeed, if it is true!' His gallantry, while she had come to expect it, could barely convince her of its sincerity, since she had no high notions of her own talent. Even so, Catherine admitted to herself that it was pleasant to be paid attention, even though she knew she must consider his praise to be elicited under the circumstances of being paid a very generous fee.

He stepped closer to her shoulder, almost brushing it with his sleeve and pointed to the lake, which she had painted in rather sombre greys and blues. 'Gloomy-looking, rather as if it were as melancholy as the artist. A hint of turbulence in the little waves, as if the artist has some secret she would rather not let surface.'

Guiltily, she laughed. 'How absurd! Perhaps that says more about the observer than the artist!'

'Perhaps it does,' he replied with a slight smile, 'but we all have secrets of some sort, do not we, Mrs Tilney?'

'Does not everyone have secrets?' she replied, blushing.

'True. But I should like to think that you might trust me with yours, since I have found you out. Is it not pleasant to relieve the burden of carrying thoughts and feelings we cannot share with others?'

"Her subject was a watercolor
scene with a lake and trees."

'But you have not found me out at all, for I have no secrets, Mr Longstaff.'

'Very well, if you insist upon it.' He chuckled and said in a low tone so as not to allow Jenny to overhear, 'Tell me, how have you managed at housekeeping these last weeks? I hope you were not taken to task too severely by your husband over the poor lost cravats?'

'No, indeed, I was not!' she replied earnestly. 'It is very kind of you to enquire after me, but Henry was very forbearing, more so than I deserved, I collect! I ought not have bothered you with my troubles, in any case.' She coloured, aware of his gaze upon her.

'Then I am glad for your sake, and it was no bother to me at all. And may I say, if you will forgive my impertinence, that perhaps your husband would do to be a little more at home in future, for I cannot imagine it is easy to be thrust into a situation, as a newly married young lady, with only a few servants to keep you company. But then, perhaps you have sisters upon whom you can rely for advice, or an old married friend who can guide you?'

'Oh, no,' replied Catherine, rather embarrassed that he had hit upon her feelings so exactly, 'there is no one — no one except Henry, I mean — and there is Mrs Poulter, the housekeeper — but —' She stopped self-consciously, for she did not mean to complain to someone who was not an intimate friend of the family.

'— but she is intimidating, and seems to watch your every move, and disapproves of your lack of experience.'

'How did you —?' Catherine was astonished.

'Oh, it is the oldest story in the book, you know. It was not hard to guess at your predicament. I have seen the way she looks at you, and it is quite impertinent, if you don't mind me saying so. It must be a trial to your nerves, and testimony to your excellent character to be so forbearing under such circumstances.'

'Forbearing? But —'

'Just so, Mrs Tilney. It really is too bad of Mr Tilney to not be more attentive to your situation. But I am sure he does not *mean* to neglect you on purpose; I am sure he would be here to guide you if he could.'

'Neglect me? Oh, no! I mean, I am sure he would be home more, but he is much occupied as the parish is a such large one.'

Would Henry be home more if there was less for him to do? She had not thought of it before. Was his being away such long hours really because he had so much to do, or was he ashamed and disgusted with her after all?

'Still,' continued Longstaff, intent now on his subject, 'it does not meet all my ideas of gallant behaviour to a female of youthful inexperience and sensitivity as yourself. But there, do not be cross with me, Mrs Tilney, for I mean no harm. Your husband, I am sure, is a very good sort of gentleman; he was certainly so to your sister, when I had the pleasure some years ago, of giving her lessons in drawing. I knew Mr Tilney then a little, and he seemed very attentive to Miss Tilney. He must not be accused of being anything remiss to yourself, I am sure!'

Doubt must have shown on her countenance, for Longstaff gave her a look of extreme pity and sympathy. He said warmly, in the kindest tones, 'Pray, don't distress yourself, Mrs Tilney. I am sure your husband is as anxious for your happiness as any man would be, with a wife as lovely and young as you are. You must not let my cynical speeches influence you! I am a man of the world, you know, and have seen many things, but of course you know best what is right and proper between you and your husband. I only meant to give comfort.'

'I— I did not mean to give the impression of *neglect*, exactly,' replied Catherine falteringly. 'I would not use so strong a word. Only — well, sometimes Henry is gone for long hours, and I confess I am used to a large, noisy company — I come from a large family, you see, so I have not been forced by circumstance to find the resources for being in my own company for long periods. It is only my own fault, I am sure, for not learning to tolerate solitude when I was at home. We children were always together, and I could certainly never find a moment away from my younger brothers, unless I was to climb a tree!'

'Climb a tree, is it? I'm afraid I cannot imagine such a thing, for you are too pretty and graceful to be boyish, I collect. There I have made you blush, and I never meant to, you know! Now I am partial to the odd tree myself, or was so as a boy. There is no more felicity to be had in the world than to be out of doors and up a tree, and if I had had children, they would all know the joys of climbing a tree, I assure you!'

Her laugh was strained, but she did not like his style of gallantry, for she was sure it was artifice and flattery, although to what point, she could not conjecture. He said nothing more, but the look of his countenance was all pity and sympathy for one so misunderstood, and so unfairly treated. She did not want pity, but it was pleasant, she admitted, to be understood. The power of a kind word when she was feeling quite low in spirits, was welcomed.

A breeze sprung up and she shivered. Longstaff gallantly bent to retrieve her shawl, which had dropped to the ground. 'Here, you must put this around you,' he said in the most solicitous manner. 'I see you are fatigued, Mrs Tilney; you must do me the favour of going inside. You must not catch a cold!' His hands lingered perhaps a second or two longer than they ought to have, but she was so grateful for his solicitude when she was feeling so low in spirits, that she passed this off as his intending to be kind.

'Yes. I mean, I do not think I shall catch cold, but all the same, I had better go inside. Good day, Mr Longstaff.'

She pondered his words, and did not like the conclusion she came to, for she had not felt as if Henry had deliberately neglected her, until today. But the seeds of discontent had been planted, watered, and now had begun to thrive, and it was some time before she could turn her mind to other things. She remained in low spirits for the rest of the day, fancying herself forgotten and an encumberment at Woodston, until her husband came home from his duties. Then, his affection seeming real, and *her* attentions and interests all his own, that she for the moment forgave Henry all the unbecoming motives she had been disposed to attribute him, and was for the time being, tolerably content.

Ten

The little anxieties and vexations of common life soon began to succeed her uncommon fears for herself and Henry, and they settled into a routine of sorts. The weather continued fine, although the days were crisp and cold, and Catherine walked to the village only when she could be sure of not having a red nose by the time she got there. Mr Longstaff continued his visits, although Catherine's paintings, she thought, were little more than watery "dabbings and dawbings" as Henry teased her. However, Longstaff was charmingly obliging and said a great deal more than he needed in the way of compliments, which she knew better than to take seriously, but still, it was pleasant to have the easy companionship which had sprung up between them when Henry was away so much.

Catherine began to long for letters from home, quite impatient to hear from her brother James, who had gone back to Oxford to complete his studies. After his disappointment the previous year with Miss Isabella Thorpe, James had not been in good spirits for some time, and Catherine worried over him to a degree which prompted him to reassure her that he was fine, and quite gotten over Miss Thorpe — indeed, he insisted, he never thought of her, and could hardly remember two words they had spoken together. These reassurances, given in so obliging and easy a manner as to seem *too* readily given, *too* easily tossed off as nothing, Catherine did not quite feel she could trust implicitly, but she left off mentioning it and contented herself with thinking of James very often and including him in some very earnest bed-time prayers.

She was not long to be waiting for a letter from him, however, for a few days into December she and Henry were taking breakfast together when one of the servants brought in the post. Catherine was delighted when Henry handed her a letter.

She looked at the direction. 'Tis from James! At last! Oh, I am excessively glad to hear from him!' She broke the wax and opened out the letter. It was written over in small, fine letters, and across again, with enquiries as to her health and happiness, many details of his life at Oxford, some amusing accounts of his friends' escapades, and finished by way of imparting to her some interesting information.

At her several exclamations, Henry, having earnestly watched her throughout, raised enquiring brows and asked if there was bad news.

'Oh no, not bad news, but something so strange! I confess I am amazingly astonished! Only hear what James says — I will read it for you —

> *'I know you will not think badly of me, Catherine, for mentioning, it, and indeed, I don't mention it to worry you over my thinking anything at all of Miss Thorpe, but I have heard some news — perhaps it is gossip, but 'news' sounds so much better, does it not! — which I will tell you, and which you will not scruple to hear since Miss Thorpe is no longer your particular friend.*
>
> *You recall my college chum, John Thorpe, Miss Thorpe's brother whom you met in Bath last year? He has just told me of a stroke of excellent luck for their family — in particular for his sisters — for it seems a paternal aunt of theirs who was excessively rich has died, and having no living children of her own, has unexpectedly left the three Miss Thorpes five thousand pounds apiece! It is an excellent generous sum indeed, especially for such a one as Isabella, on whom it seems that providence has smiled although she can hardly deserve it.*
>
> *It is very droll, is it not Cathy, to think that once Isabella threw me off for want of money, to gain another whom she thought had better prospects, and was thrown off in turn, only now to find herself in a position where she does not have to be at all nice in her choice of a husband.*

The inscrutable workings of Our Lord are beyond my ken, I am afraid, but I cannot find it in my heart to mock, nor despise the lady, even so. I wish no evil upon her head, and I hope she will be able to find a fine husband, certainly a better sort of husband than I could have made her in the circumstance.

You see, Cathy, how composed I am become with the benefit of a year's reflection. I congratulate myself on achieving such a degree of composure! I am not bitter about the matter, not at all. It was, I concede, a heavy blow at the time but as you see, I write, walk, drink, eat and live with my heart fully intact, and now can find only a hearty amusement in the way life tumbles and tosses us about. Is it not vastly diverting, to know that your old friend, after all her deceits and unprincipled ways, has now been rewarded a fortune to command, and which may keep her well enough even if she chooses not to marry?

Do write to me at once and tell me you are as amused as I have been at this piece of news! Life is ever a peculiar animal, is it not?

Dearest sister, you have been most fortunate in love, and perhaps, despite your loyal affection for a very unworthy brother which will urge you to a righteous vexation on my behalf, your own too-good nature will be enough to render you complacent when you read my letter. After all, you may congratulate yourself on having raised no eyebrows, broken no hearts, and compromised no moral values on your path to matrimony. Miss Thorpe, for all her new-found wealth, can never say the same.

My amiable regards and hearty good wishes to Tilney, and my enduring affections to you, my dear sister. Know me always, to be your devoted brother etc
J. M'"

Catherine, feeling everything that was proper for her brother, doubted perhaps the truth of his assertions that his heart was untouched by such a story, but even if he were still affected, it would do no good to quarrel with him over it. As for Isabelle Thorpe, Catherine was not so generous as her brother in wishing

Isabella a fine husband and she said so with a great deal of warmth to Henry. 'She did my brother a great unkindness — I can hardly understand how he can be so composed, for I cannot!' She sighed.

'You cannot wish away the good fortune of one, without affecting the two sisters,' replied Henry wisely. 'Money, you know, must be allowed to supply everything wanting when a young women cannot marry on looks alone. I believe the two younger Thorpe girls to be excessively plain. They, at least, deserve their fortunes and will use them well in getting themselves husbands.'

'Plain? Oh, yes, they are! Very plain indeed, although their manner of dress is smart and fashionable enough! But they are not as affected nor as false as their sister. I suppose you are right,' sighed Catherine. 'I cannot wish their good fortunes away. The two younger sisters haven't a jot of Isabella's cunning and deceitfulness and seemed to me very charming girls; they really are as deserving of such luck as Isabella is not! But it is still all exceedingly vexing! Isabella, the most hardened flirt society has ever been forced to frown upon, the most conniving and false specimen of the female sex, to have a fortune! Poor, poor James!'

Henry was amused. 'My little Kitty is a spitfire, I see! I have not heard you so heated since my father first refused us permission to marry, Catherine. And here was I sinking into complacence on the sure knowledge that my wife had the most amiable and generous nature of all women! But I shall allow you to be so feeling upon the topic, since it is on your brother's account you are angry, and when I know you are in general possessed of a most forgiving character.'

Catherine laughed self-consciously. 'Perhaps I *am* being too hard on Isabella, for I suppose even *she* might find it in her heart to mend her ways by and by. But it hardly seems fair, all the same. I own I cannot find it in my heart to be so easy about it as James is. When evil is rewarded by such good fortune I do not know what to think!'

'You wish your friend to be punished, and indeed she deserves punishment, but perhaps she has endured enough of it already— she can hardly hold up her head in town, nor return to Bath, now. Her credibility has been destroyed, and perhaps her sisters are her only friends in the world. She has already endured such censure as must surely restrain her from further evil, I think. Providence or divine judgement, it is not our place to suppose it right or wrong. Besides,' teased Henry, 'do not suppose providence to have finished with your friend yet; you may take comfort from the thought that perhaps Miss Thorpe may find herself an excessively disagreeable husband and be dreadfully unhappy forever more.'

Catherine smiled a little at Henry's tease, but knowing intimately her former friend's character, doubted the likelihood that Isabella might already have received enough punishment as to restrain her from further evil. She reflected that even if Isabella were to endure the most direct cuts in society, there was some doubt that she would ever be brought to any proper sense of shame. But Catherine's vexation on behalf of her brother was a little more easy after this, although it still it occupied her mind some time. It was not until bedtime, when Henry distracted her most pleasantly from her thoughts, that she ceased to wonder at how either providence or a divine hand could so reward such a cunning and scheming person as Isabella Thorpe, with five thousand pounds!

~ ~ * ~ ~

Two or three days after James's letter had done its part to further disturb Catherine's tenuous peace, a rider approached the house and handed over a note at the front door. Henry, upon receiving it shortly afterward, put down his newspaper and quickly glanced over its contents. Seconds later, he made a small exclamation.

'What can it be, Henry? Not bad news?' Catherine had set down her teacup in alarm.

'Judge for yourself,' replied Henry, 'but I cannot say that it is anything which will afford *me* a deal of pleasure. My father writes that he intends to favour us with a visit next week to enquire how we go on, and to inspect the gardens and the works on the estate. And it seems that my brother Frederick, being on leave from the regiment before his wedding, will join him.'

'But that is very civil of your father, is it not?' Catherine had learned that the General's motives, while quite hidden from her own understanding, were usually clear to Henry, and therefore she relied upon Henry to interpret. She added doubtfully, 'He has not yet congratulated us — I had wondered if his staying away was a sign that he did not truly approve me as your choice — but I wonder how long he will wish to stay?'

'They intend to pass two nights here. My father apologises to you for his tardiness in visiting us — wait — where is it? — ah! He says —

You may well wonder at my silence these past two months, but allow me to assure you I have been as anxious for your comfort as any father can be; in fact, I have been at some pains to give you all the peace you might wish for as new-married young people, not that but you can reasonably wish for more than a month's honeymoon, and I am content to say that in most things, both my sons are as moderate in their wishes as any father can hope for. I hear it is all the rage with young people nowadays to take a long honeymoon, but since you are so soon back at your vocation, Henry, and two months have now passed, I have not scrupled to write and inform you of my intention to call upon you and Mrs Tilney a fortnight from today, and to stay two nights at Woodston, in order to take a look over the gardens and see what cottages need attention.

Frederick is at liberty to join us and will accompany me. He has pressed me quite urgently to be one of the party, in fact, and seems as anxious as myself to make the proper civilities of a new brother-in -law, to Mrs Tilney. Mrs Tilney will be gratified, I am sure, to see how her new brother-in-law is determined to be as civil as is expected. But Fredrick is always as attentive to these things as I am myself.

As for me, I am anxious that my lengthened absence from Woodston might have had no evil effect on the gardens and buildings. I collect Henry, that you are from home quite often and will not have had the time to look over the concerns of the estate as frequently as you might

*wish. At any rate I shall be more at ease to have some time
to look them over and see what damage has been done by
the lack of attention.'*

Henry held up the letter for Catherine's inspection, but she had
not the nerve to run an eye over the rest of the note. Indeed, she
could not have been more astonished, and not a little dismayed. She
had felt herself long disliked by the General, for the best of reasons,
since on her visit the previous year to Northanger she had let slip to
Henry that she had suspected his father of some foul play
concerning the deceased Mrs Tilney, Henry's mother. Mortified by
Henry's set down, she had apologized almost at once, and felt
herself silly and young, and had never again let her imagination take
over her reason, but, while Henry had put to rest such fears, she still
felt that the General harboured some resentment of her, either
because he had guessed her assumptions and his pride had been
injured by her rudeness, or if not that, then he in all probability still
resented her for not being the rich heiress he had once thought her.

While he must now be considered family, and acquitted of the
heinous crimes she had thought him capable of over a year ago,
the General was still one of the people most capable of making
her nervous in his company. Catherine said ingenuously and quite
earnestly, 'Still, it is a very kind letter, a kind letter indeed, to
express so much anxiety on our account. I thought he did not
approve me, but I am less anxious now that he has mentioned his
deliberately staying away to give us time to settle into Woodston
as a married couple.'

Henry smiled. 'How quick you are to attribute only good
motives when there is so little excuse for it; but I collect it makes
you a better person than me, for I cannot see the same
harmlessness in his reasoning. But don't let my cynicism rub off
on you, my love; you have a kinder heart than do I and it is one of
the reasons I love you.'

'You don't believe his reason for staying away then? You think
it is because he disapproves of our marriage, even after he has given
his permission?' The inexplicability of the General's conduct had
long been food for Catherine's thoughts, but she had never been
able to make out his character other than he made her nervous and
she felt that he did not much approve of her even now.

'I cannot answer with confidence. I shall leave that to your powers of discernment,' replied Henry. 'As for Frederick's desire make up one of the party, I own I cannot account for it. As a rule, Frederick never comes to Woodston; he previously has declared it the dullest place on earth! What he can be about in coming, I cannot begin to guess at. You must have made an impression upon him, Catherine!'

'I! When he knows my feelings! — but if Captain Tilney is disposed to wish us well, then I should not like to be uncivil. Perhaps it is a sign that has really turned over a new leaf and is wishing to make amends?'

Henry laughed. 'And so it must be, for there can be no other motive, no other design, than something which turns Frederick's character suddenly to an appearance of good, at least!'

Catherine was not quite convinced of Frederick Tilney's not being able to change, but she conceded. 'Perhaps you are right, but whatever motive drives them both, they are to come to us. I suppose we will have to be giving General Tilney a very good dinner — you recall the last time when we all dined here, what a grand dinner you had to provide, and all when he said that anything would do and to go to no trouble. I never did understand your father!'

'You need not be worried, Catherine, for Mrs Poulter will take care of everything if you wish it.'

She did not hear these words without a little stab to her pride. 'Well, yes. I suppose she will,' she said with a sigh. 'But had I not best order his favourite dish, do you think? What *is* his favourite dish?'

Henry laughed. 'A fine pretty girl, preferably caught roaming an old Abbey at midnight in a diaphanous gown, and with no guardian to prevent the most unthinkable acts!' he glowered at her, his eyes casting lascivious glances over her bosom.

She blushed and tried for an admonishing tone. 'Do stop teasing, Henry! You know I am made uncomfortable every time you bring up my silliness of last year! Anyone would think *you* read more novels by Mrs Radcliffe than I ever did! And you know I have given them up entirely! I open my *History of Egypt* every day, you know!' she added demurely, if not slightly untruthfully.

'And close it again just as quickly! Now pray, don't make dagger-eyes at me! Why, did you know you are remarkably pretty when in cross looks!'

'Ooh! You are... insufferable!'

Henry relented. 'I know I am, and I should not tease. But don't mind my father's coming, Cathy; it is a sign of his good will toward us, belated though it is, and that is to be thankful for after all we have been at to get him to give his consent to our marriage.'

Catherine conceded the rightness of Henry's opinion, and in doing so endeared herself to her husband. A young girl, who has an affectionate, ingenuous heart, and few formed opinions of her own, will always be pleasing to a man, and Henry saw in Catherine's unformed mind a *tabula rasa* on which to work. To Catherine, Henry was always right, and as she was content to accept his viewpoint in most things, his devotion was fixed.

"*The afternoon brought with it a delightful surprise in the form of a letter from Fullerton.*"

Eleven

The afternoon brought with it a delightful surprise in the form of letter from Fullerton. It was rather thicker than usual, for it held, Catherine discovered, not one but several smaller notes, all penned from her brothers and sisters. Even little Georgie had written a pretty note in his large childish hand, and made her a charming drawing. Papa had written also, to which her mama had added a post-script, along with two receipts. One of these was for elderberry wine, and the other a receipt for white soup which had been Catherine's favourite on the irregular occasion her father had entertained guests at Fullerton.

Catherine read through her letters with great delight, conceived a very pleasant notion, then waited for Henry to return home. At four o' clock he came in and giving him a quarter of an hour to go to his desk, she found him at work in the library. She went to him obediently for a kiss, then said, 'I have had such a good notion, I only hope you will like it!'

Henry lifted his eyes to view her flushed countenance, raised his brows and replaced his pen into the ink well. 'What is it Catherine? Have you been solicited by another lover? A proposal of marriage, perhaps? Your cheeks are blooming such a colour as I have not seen before!' he teased.

'Of course not!' cried Catherine, laughing despite her vexation. 'How could you say such a thing! Sometimes, Henry Tilney, you are so strange! No, indeed, only I have had letters from home.'

'Ah! Then considering the colour in those cheeks, if you are not violently in love, I can only surmise that one, or perhaps all, of your siblings has solicited for an invitation to visit Woodston this very week and you are embarrassed to ask me for you know we have only room for five guests, and your brothers and sisters number nine, without counting your good father and mother!'

He was laughing and she set her mouth in a stern line. 'Don't tease me so, Henry! You know it isn't fair!'

'But nothing in the world advances familiarity as much as a tease — and you do want us to be familiar with each other, do you not?' He was still smiling.

Catherine immediately thought of his past attachment to Miss Parkhurst, and could not help feeling a little resentful that in becoming more "familiar" with herself, he had not thought to share with Cathy that he had once been in love with someone else. Then she chided herself for small-mindedness. 'What an excessive quiz you can be!' she smiled. 'But will you hear me or do you insist on making me blush?'

'Certainly I shall hear you.'

'I have had a very good notion; I want to make the dinner for your father and Captain Tilney, and have guests! That is, I don't mean to make the entire dinner, of course — Cook may do that well enough — but I propose to make the white soup myself!'

Henry looked as if she had said she wished to put on some men's pantaloons and ride her horse astride. 'Whatever for, Catherine? You've no need to impress me, I assure you, you silly goose!'

'No, no!' she exclaimed. 'Only it is the best notion in the world! If I can arrange the dinner and show Mrs Poulter that I am not so hopeless as she imagines I am, then perhaps she will — well, perhaps I will feel a little more confident, and I will learn ever so much about housekeeping and cooking and such things, too! And if your father can see how good a housekeeper I am for you, then perhaps he will be more disposed to approve of us, do not you think? You must agree it is an excellent scheme, Henry, you simply must!'

Henry exhaled and eyed his wife. He shook his head in mock despair. 'How can I deny you, Catherine, when you are so wild for it! But I am sure you don't need to prove anything to my father.'

'But I do want him to *like* me! And feel I must prove to

everyone that I am not so young and silly that I cannot make a perfectly nice dinner!'

'Ah. There is that word again! By "nice" I must suppose you mean the prettiest table, or the most tasty dishes?' He smiled. 'But I have already taken you to task for improper use of the English language when we were together in Bath, and I cannot in good faith do it again. I shall allow you to claim the word for your own use, and hereafter I shall always default to your meaning. If you say I am "nice" in my sermons, or "nice" in my dress, I shall know how to understand you! What other word in the English language has come to stand for so many different meanings as the word "nice"? But as my sister Eleanor has accused me, I am "more nice than wise" — was that not what she said of me? — and I must endeavour to improve myself.'

'You know I meant nothing of the sort! And you *are* wise, or you seem so to *me*, at any rate,' Catherine said earnestly.

'Commendation indeed! How can I deny you anything with such flattery to swell my head? If you wish to be in charge of a dinner and to make up the soup, then after such kind praise I cannot think to deny you. By all means arrange the dinner, my love. But are you sure you can manage?'

'Of course I can manage it; all I ever did at home was help Mama to make suet puddings and apple pies for the poor and infirm — I always did the stirring and I know very well how to make white soup, which we *must* have if we are to give a dinner — Mama has sent me the receipt, so I shall know just how to go on!'

While Henry suffered pangs of doubt as to the wisdom of this scheme, he could not find it in himself to deny her this chance to ingratiate herself with his father and Mrs Poulter, and said so. 'But, whom in the world can you be thinking of inviting? Whom have you decided upon as victims of your cooking?' he teased.

'Why, your sister and Lord Torrington, if you will have them. They are not so far away that they could not come and stay for a few days. Do you think we may invite them? I so want to see dear Eleanor again, and I know you do, too!'

Henry gave his laughing consent and it was agreed that Catherine would inform Mrs Poulter that Catherine herself would be in charge of the dinner for Tuesday fortnight.

'With your father and Captain Tilney, and Eleanor and Lord Torrington, and you and I, that makes a nice — I mean a *proper* — number of six. I shall write to Eleanor immediately, but you must put in a post-script, Henry, so that Lord Torrington understands the invitation comes from you! It would be very improper, would it not, if the invitation came only from me? I never know how these things ought to be done!' Catherine remarked doubtfully.

'I believe we are on intimate enough terms with my sister,' smiled Henry, 'that we needn't stand upon such ceremony, but I shall gladly add a postscript if you think it more proper.'

Catherine once again silently thanked providence for such an amenable husband and retired to write the note to her sister-in-law. If there was anyone Catherine would most like to see, it was Henry's sister, who had been a friend to her since they had met in Bath the previous year. Now recently married and made into a Viscountess, Eleanor Tilney had made a match for which she hadn't dared to hope. She had been forbidden to marry by the General, on account of her lover's lowered circumstances in life, until the gentleman had been suddenly conferred a title upon the death of a relative and had become the heir to a very sufficient income. The General had immediately sanctioned the match and Eleanor had married her sweetheart.

To Catherine, it signified little that Eleanor was now become Lady Torrington. Of more importance to her, in the course of this past year, was that Eleanor had become to Catherine a beloved sister in the truest sense of the word. Catherine had sisters and brothers aplenty at Fullerton, of course, but a year of being much acquainted with Henry's sister had brought both females to think as highly as they could of the other. There was no jealousy, no petty slights, no disharmony which ever passed between them, only good humour, and real sisterly affection. The acquaintance had passed beyond its bounds and progressed to every graduation of warm tenderness and solicitous regard for the other. They could not bear to be much apart, and even while Henry had been banned from Catherine's company for much of their separation before the General had given his consent to the union, Eleanor and Catherine had taken great pains to be meeting at least three or four times in a year which would have otherwise been an unbearable misery to them both.

Catherine now gladly wrote to Eleanor, and Henry added a post-script, begging them to come. She was rewarded in due course with a return letter.

> *Torrington House, Guildford*
> *December 8, 1798*
>
> *My dearest Catherine, whom I am fortunate enough to be able to call 'sister',*
>
> *You are very good to ask Torrington and me to stay at Woodston when you have only been in your own establishment for a short time, but I confess I have been eager to receive word that I might come to you and Henry. John has begged to be excused, for he must leave for town tomorrow and will be away for three weeks, but if you will have me, I shall be glad to come! As for my father, I can only express my gladness that he seems to have softened to the extent that he wishes to present himself at Woodston. I shall look forward to spending some time with you and Henry. It shall be just as in the old days when we were all together at Northanger!*
>
> *I confess, Catherine, I am also glad to hear that my brother Frederick will be there, for there is a matter of some importance, and some delicacy, on which I wish to speak with him, and your invitation affords me the opportunity to do so without alerting my father by an unsolicited visit to Northanger. You shall hear more from me on the subject when I come to you, but for now, pray don't mention it to Henry. He will hear soon enough, I collect. Expect me Tuesday next, at two o'clock, and until then believe me steadfastly to be your loving sister*
>
> *E. Torrington.*

Catherine was disappointed that Lord Torrington could not be of the party, which would now make uneven numbers at table, but she was somewhat relieved that she would, for a few days at any rate, have some company other than her own. As to what Eleanor had hinted at with regard to Frederick, she was quite mystified. Woodston seemed more and more full of secrets, and Catherine the only one who did not understand them!

Mrs Poulter was informed of the expected party of visitors to Woodston and took the news blandly. As for being informed that Catherine herself would make the soup, she could barely comprehend it.

'It is never done, Mrs Tilney — the mistress of the house making the soup? Whatever next? Cleaning out the chamber pots of a morning? Setting the fires with Emily?'

Perhaps,' said Catherine with unusually daring spirit, 'these are the things I ought to be learning, Mrs Poulter — I am hardly yet able enough to run a house, and I cannot bear it if people think I am merely a fine lady, not fit for anything but indolence and indulgence!'

'I would never have accused you of being a *fine* lady, Ma'am,' remarked the housekeeper blandly, and Catherine was much put upon to retain her dignity at the veiled insult. 'However, there are varying degrees of refinement to be found in any society. It is hardly a requirement for a young wife, unless she is from a *lower* class, Ma'am, to prepare food.' Mrs Poulter looked Catherine up and down with a cold disapproval.

For all Catherine's agreeable temper and tendency to cheerfulness in general, she felt the impudence of the woman deeply. However, she held her tongue in check and was not to be thwarted in her scheme. 'I do not suggest that I make the *entire* dinner, Mrs Poulter, only the soup. Is it not sometimes done in homes where servants number fewer than what is needed to prepare a large dinner? Mama always helped cook at home, and although I was a very poor student indeed, it is never too late to learn how to run a home, surely?'

Catherine had not expected that Mrs Poulter would easily be able to bring herself to agree with this scheme but the older woman at last appeared to understand the futility of arguing, especially if Mrs Tilney had the approval of the master, and beyond prophesying disaster privately to Jenny later, did not openly give further opposition.

Still, she eyed Catherine with distrust. 'Well I never! I would have thought, Ma'am, that visiting the sick and poor and doing flowers for church, was all the expectation for any clergyman's wife. Mr Tilney may not be vastly wealthy, but there are servants enough here to do those tasks your mother may not have had servants for.' She regarded Catherine with a supercilious eye. 'But seeing as how you seem so enthusiastic for it, Ma'am, I should not like to step in the way of a good intention. Let us hope your scheme doesn't go the same way the cravats did! Well, I suppose you might ask Cook to teach you the soup, if Mr Tilney is in agreement of course,' she added pointedly.

'Mr Tilney is in *perfect* agreement,' replied Catherine rather sharply, colouring deeply at the mention of the cravats. 'But I already have Mama's own receipt for the soup. I have made it with Mama before,' she added, not quite truthfully, because stirring the pot, she conceded, was not exactly making the soup, but she had the receipt, so she was certain it could not be quite so hard as Mrs Poulter was inclined to have her believe.

She ordered a suckling pig, which Henry had told her was General Tilney's favourite dish, and a venison, which was Henry's, and gave her approbation for any and all other dishes the housekeeper thought necessary. Feeling very much as if she had made a new start in being the useful wife she wished to become, Catherine remained in a cheerful mood for the rest of the day.

She did not mention Mrs Poulter's insolent remarks to Henry, knowing a successful soup must be all that was needed to put Mrs Poulter in her place. General Tilney would regard her with a new respect, Henry would see that she was capable of being a good parson's wife after all, and she herself would have no need to feel herself an encumberment at Woodston. With her heart in the right place, and armed with what little knowledge she had on the business of making a white soup, Catherine had nothing left to do but hope that all her plans would have the desired outcomes.

"She spent all Sunday afternoon perusing the ingredients, consulting with Cook, and gathering various items for her soup."

Twelve

There is an old adage, that 'anyone who tells a lie has not a pure heart; and therefore cannot make a good soup.' It must follow then, that Catherine, possessing her mother's own receipt and as honest a heart as any, could not fail of producing a good soup. The dish was duly begun, a full two days before anyone of the visiting party was expected.

After attending service and listening dutifully to her husband's sermon, she spent all Sunday afternoon perusing the ingredients, consulting with cook, and gathering various items for its manufacture. She brought to the task so much earnestness, so much intention for doing good, so much zeal to the activities of chopping up onions and carrots, looking over the veal with cook and approving it — although she had no notion of what was good or a bad piece — that if the outcome were based on enthusiasm alone, she could not have failed. The veal was boiled, the herbs added with care, and as many sugared almonds as were called for in her mother's receipt disposed of by way of her plump red mouth as went into the pot.

Cook, who was a deal more amenable than Mrs Poulter, was wary at first, but when she perceived Catherine's keen interest she relented and became almost helpful, although Catherine demanded that she be allowed to do most of the preparations herself. With the woman's help, however, Catherine was able to produce what Cook declared to be 'an excellent broth', and she finished the task with almost as much confidence as when she had begun it.

Mrs Poulter had absented herself from the proceedings, for which Catherine was grateful, but even Henry, anxious for Catherine's success, on venturing down to the kitchen end of the house to see how things were progressing was unceremoniously shooed away as readily as Peggy the kitchen cat.

'Go write your sermons,' cried Catherine, laughing. 'You may have some on Tuesday and not before!'

'Cruelty, indeed, but I see how it is to be from now on. I shall have no say in anything, and must become content to be ordered about by my wife!' But his countenance spoke amusement and he retired to his study rather less anxious than he had left it.

Much elated at her own success, Catherine left the soup cooling in the larder, carefully covered in layers of damp muslin, awaiting consumption.

Catherine had been looking for Tuesday with both dread and eagerness, for it was to be her first dinner of importance since she had become mistress of Woodston. Time seemed to lumber, and Monday seemed never to come to a close, but nevertheless, Tuesday arrived, perfectly on time, and with it brought Eleanor. There was a little fluster of embraces and kisses and animated conversation between the three of them, for Henry had come home early on purpose to greet his sister.

Eleanor was everything kind, modest and sweet, and soon had Catherine feeling that no time at all had passed since they last were together. But the three of them had not had above half an hour together, each eager to hear every account of the other, before another carriage rolled up in state, and the General and Captain Tilney entered the drawing room shortly afterward.

All the party seemed in good spirits and in general disposed to be pleased with each other. A warming glass of negus was served, which had the effect of rendering Catherine only slightly less anxious that something should not go wrong! Even so, she was at first inclined to be overpowered by General Tilney, embarrassed and vexed in Captain Frederick Tilney's presence, and nervous in front of so large a party in general. Despite the sweet presence of Eleanor, who took pains to be familiar and kind, Catherine spent the first fifteen minutes among them all in a state of agitation lest she should somehow not do what was exactly right as the mistress of Woodston and lose their good opinions of her.

However, a few more minutes brought some polite, even gallant, civilities from the General on the subject of his having refrained from visiting them sooner on account of his having wished to give them time alone. There followed some gracious remarks even from Captain Tilney on the same topic, and Catherine was made almost easy in their company, with the support of Henry's arm. She had put on her best white spotted muslin, and taken pains with her hair, conscious of making a good impression.

Captain Tilney appeared to Catherine's eye to be as sly as he ever was, his gaze never seeming to contain that candour which had drawn her to his siblings. He was quiet, said very little as a rule, and appeared discontented. When he did speak, it was to utter some drawling, clever remark, but although his lips curved upwards in a smile from time to time, the smile never reached his eyes. Catherine was exceedingly curious as to the possibility of a man such as Captain Tilney being capable of truly giving his heart to another, but when she hesitantly enquired of the lady whom he was to marry, he spoke of his nuptial partner with little warmth.

She was a Miss Sweeting, he told them, of a good family in Wiltshire, an heiress with the dual advantage of a both pretty face and a tolerable fortune. She was possessed of one brother who had inherited the family estate, but she had three years ago removed to live with an infirm aunt in Somerset, where she would reside until her marriage. 'We have been forced to delay the union somewhat, due to the ill health of the aunt with whom she lives, and to whom Agnes is devoted. I cannot see how that must affect our own schemes so directly, but one must keep one's future wife happy, I suppose. It is all a dreadful bore to me,' he added with a slight smile. 'However, I have stipulated to Agnes that we must return to Northanger a married couple by the new year.'

Eleanor now remarked gently, 'It shows a very pleasing regard, a very creditable devotion on the lady's part for a beloved aunt. I am sure she is doing everything that is proper and due her aunt, Frederick. After all, are not devotion to duty, and real affection and esteem, the very qualities one might reasonably look for in a wife?'

Henry laughed. 'Eleanor, pray do not forget to whom you speak. There will be some men with whom such qualities are held in the highest regard and may constitute those under which they would condition to marry, but my brother cannot afford to be so nice; he can forgo such an excellent character, if only he is compensated by a tolerable pretty face and an adequate fortune. Is it not so, Fred?'

Captain Tilney concurred with a sly smile. 'You, Henry, need not have a very handsome income as you live modestly, in a humble parsonage, and even if you were heir to a grand fortune, you are limited as to spending it, since you must be an example in the parish. I, on the other hand, must bear the burden which falls to the eldest son, and therefore it is my duty to our father to ensure Northanger is not neglected in my lifetime. A very pretty wife surely is not an unreasonable demand in compensation for being obliged to marry a fortune.'

'Obliged!' cried Henry in mock despair but his father was too beforehand and cut him off.

'Hear, hear!' he cried from his seat opposite. 'Frederick never forgets what is owing to me, and to his birthright.'

'Then you would not take an ugly wife?' Henry enquired of Frederick with a smile.

'My eyes take pleasure in a sweet and youthful countenance, in a blooming cheek, and are repelled by a rugged one. If I am obliged to marry only for fortune, then I must at the very least stipulate for a pretty wife. My taste *must* have satisfaction.'

Eleanor said composedly, 'Then I can only beg you that added to her beauty, you will give me a sister-in-law who will satisfy my own taste — and Henry's and Catherine's too, I vouchsafe to say — one who is devoted, artless, kind, affectionate, and dutiful. I have already such a sister-in-in law, it is true,' she added, giving Catherine the fondest glance, 'but to add such another, how I should delight in my fortune!'

Henry added, 'I take great hopes, Fred, in her namesake; I believe it to be a great sign! She should be "sweet" to us all, indeed!'

Frederick, applied to thus, could not give them all much more information as to Miss Sweeting's character, but added only that as he had often observed that nine out of ten husbands lived to be plagued in their choice of a wife, and that all females hid their true natures as long as the engagement lasted, that they must all wait at least a day after his marriage took place, before he could answer for the degree of amiability they could expect from his wife.

Henry and Eleanor laughed at this, but Catherine thought it quite cynical although she would not say so. General Tilney, however, was more gallant and could not allow it to be so, and made some pretty compliments to the lady in question. Then the discussion of marriage was forfeited in favour of the General's interests in Woodston. The topic of the improvements he had planned for the garden was raised and exhausted; to Cathy it was a confusing discussion of roofing and heating pipes, manure and hot houses, and a new tropical fruit called a "man-go", of which she had never heard, and the cultivation of which interested her far less than it did the others.

Instead, she had been thinking of her former friend Isabella while Captain Tilney had been speaking, and had been obliged to marvel at her own folly only a few weeks ago, in supposing Captain Tilney to be in love. Of course, he must marry a fortune — *that* could excite no surprise. It was, she supposed, his undeniable duty to his father, as heir. She could not despise him so greatly as she had last year, although she still harboured some ill-feeling for the inadvertent abuse of her brother's heart. But she could not excuse him the great disservice he did to women in general! Her own romantic notions of marriage had been formed at a young age, and notwithstanding the number of novels upon the subject which she had voraciously devoured in her youth, she had also the example set by her own mother and father, who were as in harmony after twenty years of marriage as they had been after one!

The conversation soon turned to talk of Northanger, and the General turned to Henry and said, 'You will wish to know, Henry, that I have made some not insignificant progress in the investigations which have been taking place regarding the missing items from your mother's rooms at Northanger. My man of business has mentioned the name of a pawn shop where the items were said to have been presented to the proprietor for exchange — a pretty sum was demanded for them, too — but upon seeing that the items were of a quality not likely to be naturally gotten by such an ill-dressed fellow, the proprietor suspected almost immediately that they were stolen and would not have them. The fellow was told to take them away, and did so. I have had my man make enquiries and hope soon to be able to make certain of the fellow's identity which may, with some enquiries, lead to the whereabouts of the jewellery.'

Eleanor lifted her eyes to Captain Tilney's. 'I hope for your sake, Frederick, and for Catherine's too, that my mother's keepsakes might be recovered. She would be sad, indeed, to think she could not have given to your bride what she would willingly have given if she were still alive.'

'What Miss Sweeting does not know will give her no discomfort,' drawled Captain Tilney. 'You have your mother's things already, Eleanor; it is hardly any concern of yours to worry for Henry and me. I dare say they will be discovered in the bottom of some drawer, put away and forgotten, or has anyone searched the servants' quarters again?'

'It is very dreadful, is it not,' declared Catherine to Eleanor in feeling tones, 'to think of trusted servants at Northanger, in your father's house, who would show such disregard for your mother's memory, when it is likely that they knew her and served her! And then to do such a wicked thing!'

Eleanor could only give Catherine a sad smile, and the subject having been canvassed quite more than it ought to have been for Eleanor's comfort, they soon afterwards they quit the room to take their dinner.

Thirteen

General Tilney looked over the dinner table with a critical eye as they entered the dining room. Catherine had been nervous, lest he should find fault with the decorations — perhaps they were too effusive — or the plate not elegant enough — but he seemed to find nothing amiss, and Catherine sighed her relief.

The dining room was large, commodious, and handsomely fitted up, the General himself having done over the room for Henry's sake when he had japanned. 'Although we are not calling it a splendid room,' he remarked. 'It cannot be compared to Northanger, naturally. But still, I believe it is one of the better-sized dining rooms in the country. But Mrs Tilney, I have seen no sign of your improving hand at Woodston; you must be quite eager to mould it to your own refined taste.' As Catherine began her embarrassed protests, he added, 'I think you *must* see that the room waits only for a lady's discerning taste — indeed you must choose some new papers and hangings, for I am sure you have only restrained yourself from affecting such a change due to a modest disinclination for exercising your own discerning tastes. It would not do, I agree, to display that elegance of living which might make a mockery of your husband's profession, but remember that the Tilney family is certainly expected — there is a certain style of living — in short, I think you may make some changes here without incurring any disgust.'

Captain Tilney said drily, 'Or perhaps Mrs Tilney fears giving offence to your taste, Sir, by expressing a desire of changing anything.'

Catherine, who had thought no such things, hardly knew what to reply to such gallantry without offending the General. But the dishes were just now being bought in and the wine set upon the side table. Emily and Jane had begun to go around the table with it, and Catherine now leaned toward Eleanor who was seated on her left and said in a low voice, 'I must confess, Eleanor, that I am in a great anxiety to have everyone like the white soup!'

Eleanor gave her an enquiring glance. 'I am sure it is excellent. Henry's cook is a very decent one, equal to any dish, I collect! You ought not be in so much anxiety about it, dearest!'

'Oh, no, but you see, I have made it myself, with Mama's receipt — to prove to Henry, and your father, that I am not such a sad housekeeper as you all must think me!'

The General, overhearing these remarks, expressed his astonishment. 'Sad housekeeper! Make the soup yourself! Vastly commendable, indeed, Mrs Tilney, but there was no need on my own account — I own myself indifferent as to food, you know — it is all the same to me, although I am obliged to you for the thought.'

'Indifferent!' laughed Captain Tilney in his lazy way. 'I shall not scruple to pain your modesty with a rebuttal, Sir; you are as conscientious an epicure as I have known! I have met with you forever in town, at the oyster house in St. Martin's-lane, and as for the Piazza Coffee House at Covent Garden — such dinners as I have heard you to have given there yourself —!'

His father was quite civil in the face of such an attack. He accepted the wine being poured into his glass, tasted it at his leisure then said, 'Oh, that may be so, Frederick, but it is many months since I have visited Sawyer's — and only for the sake of my friends, you know.' Here he turned to Catherine. 'I make it an object to be obliging to my friends, Mrs Tilney, and I leave it to them entirely where we shall dine — when I am in town, I am never with them more than once in a week, and so it does not matter where and what we eat. I have been accused of neglecting my health by missing meals — but my friends see that I eat, which may say more than I could myself, about my perfect indifference as to meals.'

Catherine was unable to make much of a reply to this, her mind being much occupied with uniting two very differing ideas; the General's being "perfectly indifferent as to meals", and the opposing silent testimony made by his sizable bulk.

The General however, did not require a reply and continued on. 'But I do not talk of dishes when there is something better to talk of; you are in very good looks, Ma'am,' he added gallantly, 'if you will permit me to say so. Your figure is much filled-out, and your mode of wearing your hair, is, I think, similar to Eleanor's when you stayed with us last year.'

Henry had been quiet, allowing his father to lead, but here, perceiving Catherine's ever-rising self-consciousness, he interjected with amusement, 'I am shocked indeed, Father, to hear of your neglecting your diet so thoroughly in town, but as to my wife's being in looks, pray stop there and speak no further. You know how pretty compliments make Catherine blush. Now that she is a married lady, she does not wish to hear of her beauty or her fine figure. Married ladies, as you must know, are obliged upon marriage to give up the concerns of single females! Their concerns must be domestic only. That is why you can marry what you thought was a fine-looking girl in January and find by July that you were mistaken; she is a fat girl with a red nose!'

Catherine was unsure if she ought to protest or allow Henry's outrageous tease. 'Henry! You are teasing me again! Eleanor, we must band together. Your brother is being quite absurd! I collect he is making sport of us!'

'Aye, and I have not the power to prevent him,' replied a laughing Eleanor. 'He will not listen to his sister, married or not!'

'Then what, pray, can ingratiate us to the mistress of Woodston?' asked Captain Tilney in low, silky tones.

'I will tell you,' replied Henry gravely, 'for as a new-married lady, I collect it is a perfectly rational expectation. My wife only has her heart set upon our warm and profuse commendations for having provided you all with a perfectly-arranged table, a house whose situation and appearance exceed all others in the neighbourhood, the best dinner service next to that of Northanger, and a perfectly made white soup!'

'Indeed, I wish no such thing!' laughed a pink-cheeked Catherine. 'Well, perhaps the part about the soup, but you are very unkind to tease me in front of guests, Henry!'

'I cannot,' remarked the General, 'admit of being neglectful about white soup, for it is always on the table at Northanger — it is expected, of course, in all finer families — but even aside from that, I confess I like it to a degree, although generally I never give a moment's thought from one meal to the next, you know — one cold meat is as the next, so long as I have my fill of it, for there is nothing I dislike more than an empty table, but so long as there are one or two good dishes, I am quite easily satisfied — but how unnecessary your labour, when there are servants enough to go on with quite comfortably — but you have behaved very commendably I am sure, Madam, in making it yourself, on the occasion of our little party, all together again, eh?'

Catherine, who from a close acquaintance the previous year, and witnessing his over-bountiful dinner tables for a month straight, heard the General's protests doubtfully, and had little to reply, except a blushing, 'You are very kind, I am sure!'

Eleanor gave her a most compassionate look when the topic had turned to something else and said quietly, 'You must know that Henry does not care if you can make a dinner, or make the soup yourself, for he is too much in love with you to notice!'

'You are too kind,' whispered Catherine, 'but it is a great object with me to prove to you all I am not so ignorant as I was when I began married life!'

The soup had by now been ladled into the bowls by the servants, and the wine poured, and the party at the table began to sup. Within a few moments, however, Catherine had put down her spoon in dismay. It could not be! She had tested it herself two days ago and been perfectly satisfied with the result, but now it was salty to a degree which made it inedible. Soon the General and Captain Tilney had put down their spoons with low exclamations, and a stuttering Catherine was pink-cheeked and apologetic. 'I— I am exceedingly sorry; something dreadful must have — perhaps Cook — I can hardly say what has happened!'

Henry and Eleanor alone had forbearingly continued to eat their soup, after owning their own surprise, but even Eleanor was finally forced to rest her spoon. 'It is only a very *little* salty; perhaps a mistake was made in the kitchen, but pray do not take it to heart, dear! I am sure we shall have excellent courses to follow!'

Catherine was conscious that, despite his frequent assertions, it seemed to her that General Tilney tended to be exceedingly fastidious about his food. Therefore she eyed him with a great degree of trepidation and shame as he pushed away his plate and begged Mrs Tilney 'would not be made anxious over the mistake — he was not perturbed by it — he was careless enough in his own matters of eating, it really did not signify — perhaps it was a little salty — he would decline soup, although he was used to beginning a dinner with it — but if she had made it herself, it was only a first attempt, and he was sure she would soon make a creditable housekeeper of herself, but no matter, the small inconvenience of having no first course was probably equally attributable to the kitchen at Woodston having no modern stove such as Northanger's could boast —'

Here, Catherine was almost at the point of inadvertently adding more salt to the injury by weeping her growing vexation and shame right into the bowl in front of her. But by Henry's kind remarks, his making very little of the matter himself, and passing it off as a mistake perhaps by one of the servants, she was made tolerably composed again. The offending soup plates were removed by Jane, and more dishes laid upon the table. Order was restored, and Catherine's shame was hidden by eating her venison with as much gusto as she could summon. But she could only consume a small portion before giving in to rising shame. She could not help but be vexed beyond a moderation; perhaps it *was* a mistake by one of the servants, but she could not fail to guess which of the servants at Woodston would have done such a thing. However, she determined not to allow the incident to excite her anger into an open conflict. She would not let that odious woman make a fool of her!

Fourteen

Dinner over, the party retired to the drawing room. Catherine, still vexed and puzzled over the over-salted soup, tried for as cheerful a countenance as she could summon, but a certain pinkness in her cheeks every now and then was the only sign that she was thinking of things other than making civil conversation with the General.

After a while the conversation lagged and Henry suggested they play at Whist.

His brother at once showed a keen inclination. 'All this sitting around on a full stomach is so tiring,' drawled he. 'Eleanor, will you not be my partner against Henry and Catherine?'

But Eleanor had become suddenly quiet and would not join them, even though urged by Catherine herself. 'No indeed, I thank you. I— I am tired from my journey and will sit here instead.'

Catherine saw that Eleanor had cast a quick glance at Frederick which looked very much as if it was intended to scold, but Captain Tilney had been very busy opening his snuff box and missed his sister's pointed look. Cathy wondered briefly what Eleanor might have meant by such a glance. Was the business she had said she had with Frederick something in the way of a scolding? Catherine sighed. She would have to wait until Eleanor confided in her.

But very soon the General urged Eleanor to relieve her fatigue with a little exercise at the pianoforte. 'It is too easy, I think, to fall into dull spirits, when a change in occupation may relieve fatigue as well as rest may do.'

Eleanor immediately rose from her place on the sofa without demure to obediently oblige her father and soon the card party were listening to Eleanor entertain them at the pianoforte.

Catherine found much to admire in her sister-in-law's performance, which wanted neither taste nor spirit, and for a full quarter of an hour, between making bets and sighing over disappointing cards, she sat in humble regret at her own lack of attention to the instrument. But she was modest enough to acknowledge that such regrets with her were always fleeting, for she would still much prefer to devote her time to a novel than to practicing.

When Eleanor had favoured them with two lively Irish airs and a sonata by Clementi, she was then entreated by General Tilney to give them a song. 'I have not heard you and Henry sing together since you were last together at Northanger, Eleanor. You are quite accomplished enough, I hold, to amuse only a little family party, I think. What say you, Henry?'

'Of course, Sir, if Eleanor is not tired?' Henry turned to his sister and received a smile of assent.

Catherine exclaimed rather guiltily, 'I did not know you sang, Henry! How delightful it would be to hear you both.'

Abandoning his hand, Henry rose from the card table and immediately and went to the pianoforte. Rifling through the music there he pulled out a piece, opened it and placed it before Eleanor. 'We have not performed *Adelaide* together for an age; it would give me the most pleasure to sing it again, just as in old times.'

The others abandoned their game also and took up positions on the sofa and armchairs to properly enjoy the performance. Pretty notes swelled under Eleanor's nimble fingers, and Catherine watched and listened in growing shame as she acknowledged that she ought to have known that her husband could sing — possessed a very agreeable baritone, in fact — but even more distressing was the knowledge that it could have been herself and Henry, playing and singing as husband and wife, if it were not for her own lack of diligence. Coupled with the shame she had already suffered over dinner, seeing Henry so obviously enjoying the opportunity to sing added to her growing misery. Henry had never mentioned that he was fond of singing, and it pained her to think he had not thought to tell her. He seemed very much disposed for it, and Catherine wondered if he resented her not

"*A pleasant hour or two was passed
in listening to Eleanor entertain
them at the pianoforte.*"

being accomplished enough to accompany him. However, she composed herself well enough to join the others in giving them a deserving applause.

Captain Tilney, who had gone to stand at the window, now approached Catherine and seated himself beside her on the chaise before the fire. 'Do you often think of our time together at Bath, Mrs Tilney? It must occupy your thoughts sometimes. It was, after all, the scene of your triumph over my brother.'

Catherine did not know how to answer, given that he must know it would afford her only discomfort to speak of the place where her brother was so ill-treated at the hands of himself and Isabella Thorpe, but she said rather stiffly, 'I rather think it was your brother, Captain, who made a triumph over me! I never saw any gentleman I liked so well as Henry.'

'You made a conquest of him and rightly so; it is refreshing, and quite unusual, in such a place as Bath, I think, to find a female untouched by cynicism, not yet soured from the vexations and ironies of life. You have all the advantage of youth on your side to protect you from becoming tired of Bath. I collect you were quite wild for the place, were not you?'

'I liked it very much,' replied Catherine coolly, 'but I think any young woman would find much in its society to amuse and divert.'

'I must hold that even in Bath, all society becomes jaded and tired after a time.'

'Jaded and tired?' she cried. 'How can you say so? I did not find it had that effect on me! For the time I was there, I was quite pleasantly diverted — most of the time, that is.' She blushed. Catherine was unhappy to be talking of Bath, for the place held memories for her which were not entirely comfortable; as the scene of her beloved brother James' painful parting of ways with Isabella Thorpe, to speak of Bath was painful to her. Captain Tilney's own wicked part in the event, as Catherine judged it, made Bath an unlikely subject for her comfort.

Tilney continued. 'Perhaps you feel this way because you are young. If you were to return after a few years, it would not be nearly so amusing.'

'I hardly know if you are right or wrong, Captain. I will try the strength of that in a few years, perhaps. But I can say that my friend, Miss Thorpe, who is four years older than me, found much in Bath to amuse her. To the detriment of my brother,' she added archly, hoping to shame him into contrition.

But Captain Tilney would not be goaded. 'Ah, Miss Thorpe— I will wager that you must still correspond with the lady. You were such good friends at the time, I recollect. In fact, you were both charmingly inseparable.'

'Indeed, I do *not* correspond with her! How you could ask me about Isabella, Captain? I can hardly account for your curiosity, given the circumstances.' Catherine kept her tone low, but there was no mistaking the anger in her voice.

Captain Tilney, upon comprehending this, seemed to be put in his place. 'Forgive me, Mrs Tilney. I had only wished to speak of Bath in general terms. I hope very much your friend is good health, and that you may one day renew your friendship, despite the trying circumstances which surrounded it.'

Catherine was amazed he could still be speaking of it, and told him so. 'Besides, Miss Thorpe and I are not likely to meet again, Captain, for she has come into a great fortune and no doubt will marry well. Henry and I will likely not go to town, nor to Bath, this year, and perhaps not the next either, as his duties keep him here, and therefore I am not likely to meet Miss Thorpe again.' *Even if she had wanted to*, she thought silently, but it seemed Captain Tilney had taken her point and was withdrawing with a supercilious bow.

Soon the General announced himself tired, and it being briefly settled amongst themselves that an early night would allow for an early rising the next day in order for General Tilney to inspect the cottages and glass houses, soon the whole party had retired to their various rooms. Mrs Poulter came behind them to snuff out the candles, and Catherine had caught the woman's eye as she had accompanied Eleanor upstairs. However, if there was any trace of triumph in her countenance Catherine could not detect it in the gloom of the hallway. She resolved to be as circumspect about the incident with the soup as possible, but she determined to be ever more on her guard.

When they had gone to their own chamber, Henry had been comforting. 'Never mind the soup, my love, you cannot be expected to get everything perfectly on a first attempt; it was a decidedly well-arranged dinner, and I commend you for your first effort.'

'That would be all the praise I desired, Henry, if it were not for the fact that I left that soup tasting perfectly, and I cannot account for the sudden change in it, since leaving it on the pantry shelf for a day and a half!'

'Perhaps the salt bowl fell into the soup? Or perhaps a servant accidently dosed it with salt thinking it had not been added?'

'No, indeed,' she cried, rather vexed. 'I had been so careful! It could not have been an accident!'

Henry fixed her with a look. 'Then what is it you infer?'

'I— I am only saying that it could hardly be an accident; Cook would never have — I mean to say, I was so very careful, that I suspect it was not an accident...' She faltered.

'What can you mean to say, Catherine? Surely it was only a mistake, or perhaps you had not tasted it properly? No one in the house would have done anything deliberately, when everyone knew what store you had set in making it yourself!'

Catherine, feeling that this was just what had happened, could not help herself. 'Not everyone at Woodston has made me welcome. I have tried to fit in, to learn to be a good wife, but no matter what I do, I have been made to feel unwanted and —'

'— and from these circumstances,' interjected Henry warmly, 'you infer perhaps some mischief on the part of one of the most long-standing servants at Woodston? Some injustice to yourself based upon whatever false notions you have of someone's disapprobation of you? I think I do not need you to answer that, for I have an idea to whom you direct this accusation.'

Henry's tone was cool, cold even, and Catherine, who only wished to have the comfort of her husband's understanding and approval, for the first time felt alone and lost to him. She stood silently, not able to speak for the growing misery in her heart.

Henry continued. 'If I comprehend you rightly, you have formed a notion which I confess I am surprised at, given your behaviour last year at Northanger. There I thought you had learned to temper your irrational suspicions. I am disappointed in you, Catherine.'

Unable to refrain any longer, Catherine, with tears running down her cheeks, now cried, 'Irrational! When that woman has seemed bent on making my life a misery here, and has shamed me and humiliated me in front of the servants! You do not know! — and you are always gone! — I am left to fend for myself — you do not care how lonely it is here without you! I— I am neglected, a last thought!'

Henry stood still as if he had been struck. His cheeks were pink with anger. 'I cannot believe what you accuse Mrs Poulter of doing, and as for my absence, you knew this was my vocation before we married. I do believe you are irrational now, and overwrought. Go to bed. We will talk no more of this tonight.' He turned on his heel and was gone from the room.

It was their first true disagreement. Catherine, all anger, wretchedness and shock, sat limply upon the bed and wondered what had happened to her fairy tale marriage and her happy ever after. She had come to Woodston to be happy, but it seemed she might have made a grave miscalculation of her future, and her husband's character.

With a heavy heart she sat for some time, considering all that had passed. Perhaps there was some truth in what Henry had said; she was overwrought and perhaps a little irrational, and perhaps the soup had only been involved in an unfortunate misadventure. Although she still felt misunderstood and quite as wretched as she had felt for a long time, she decided that it had been wrong of her to make her suspicions so plain, especially since she had no evidence of Mrs Poulter's salting the soup. As for Henry's absences, it was true that she had married him with some understanding of his vocation, for she was, after all, a clergyman's daughter, although her father had never been quite as from home as Henry was. Mr Longstaff's recent words came rushing back to her, and she was instantly ashamed of herself for saying them aloud. Henry did not really neglect her, but she did own that sometimes she felt a little resentful to be left alone so much.

Fifteen

Catherine undressed miserably and got into bed. After a time, she heard the clock strike midnight. Henry had not returned. Cathy had been raised under the great biblical admonition never to let the sun set on a disagreement and knowing she would be unable to sleep until she had made her peace with him, she determined to go in search of him and beg his favour again. She threw a warm wrap about her shoulders, fetched her candle, and crept to her door. Henry was most likely in his study, and she opened her door with the intention of going downstairs directly to find him.

As she crept quietly into the dark passageway, however, she perceived a faint light under the door of Captain Tilney's chamber. Low voices issued from within the room.

How odd, she thought, and crept a little closer. With some surprise she detected Eleanor's voice, soft and gentle but clear, and Captain Tilney's own male one, from time to time answering his sister. It seemed as if they were having a sort of disagreement, for Eleanor's tone was urgent, even while it was soft. Cathy detected low her murmurs, and then suddenly Captain Tilney's voice was clear and as urgent as Eleanor's.

'If you tell Father, Eleanor, it will all be over for the me. Miss Sweeting is not so foolish as to go ahead with the marriage if she discovers —' and then his voice was lost once more behind the door.

Catherine, feeling ashamed for listening in, moved away from the room and crept toward the top of the stairs. If Captain Tilney and his sister were having some kind of disagreement, then they were in good company with herself and Henry. She wondered what it was that Captain Tilney did not want Miss Sweeting to discover. Whatever it was, it must be serious. How strange that they should all be at odds with each other. It had been a most upsetting night altogether.

She went quietly down the stairs and was nearing the hallway when she was suddenly held motionless by a sudden noise from below. She snuffed out her candle — most irrationally, she thought to herself, for she was in her own home, cheerful Woodston, where nothing crept in the corridors of a night except the odd mouse. Still, she froze in place. She was only just in time, for as she pressed herself to the wall halfway down the stairs, she commanded a view of the hallway stretching down to the kitchen, and midway along that hallway the door to the cellar was opening slowly outwards, just visible in the gloom of the passage.

Catherine almost screamed, such as was her astonishment, but when a familiar figure stepped out from the door into the dark hall she recognized the form and stood very still.

Mrs Poulter stepped into the hall, carrying a lantern. As she stepped into the hallway there was slight noise from the library opposite and Mrs Poulter quickly closed the cellar door, not locking it behind her in her haste to retreat down the hall unseen. However, the most puzzling thing to Catherine was that the housekeeper carried nothing with her; no bottle was brought up at all. It was, Catherine thought, excessively strange that the housekeeper should need to be in the cellar at this time of night, and not even to bring up bottles of wine. For what purpose had she been downstairs, and why did the woman move so quietly, as if she wished to hide?

Mrs Poulter had proceeded hastily toward to the kitchen, and most likely, thought Catherine, up the back stairs to the servants' rooms on the third floor. Once the flickering light of the woman's lantern had vanished, Catherine continued on downstairs, careful to make no noise. Henry's study was off the library, and so she made her way to the library door which had been left open. Sure enough, there was a faint light beneath the door to Henry's study, and

Catherine was just about to enter the library, when the study door opened, and Henry himself came out.

Catherine had now been subject to so much which had taxed her nerves that she instinctively moved into the gloom of the hallway again and pressed herself into an alcove. Without knowing why, she stood there, terrified lest her husband should discover his wife hiding in her own house. But her fears were unfounded, for Henry passed directly across the hall, not noticing Catherine pressed into the wall behind him. He opened the cellar door and disappeared down into its cavernous darkness.

Nothing could describe Catherine's consternation and she stood for some minutes, unsure if she ought to be following Henry downstairs. Why would Henry visit the wine cellars so late at night? But fearing his anger if she followed him, she thought it best to wait, and in a few minutes he had appeared again, his own flickering candle announcing his arrival before she heard his feet on the steps. Moments later he emerged, and Catherine saw with some surprise, by the faltering light of his candle, that he had in his hand something which looked, to her rising astonishment, very like the handkerchief and ring she had found in the chest. Henry disappeared back into the library and seconds later Catherine heard the study door close quietly.

For all her foolish imaginings at Northanger the year before, what she had seen this night, before her eyes, was more alarming than anything she could ever have imagined in her youth. Her surmise that Mrs Poulter had hidden the items below had now at once to be dismissed, for a great truth had now made itself apparent, and all she had not wished to contemplate now struck her with some force of conviction; the 'P' of the initials on the handkerchief in the cellar did not, she was convinced, stand for "Poulter" after all, but for "Parkhurst!"

Shock of the greatest degree overcame her, and with it, a wretched misery. Henry still loved Miss Parkhurst; it must be so! Why else would he have hidden trinkets from her, keepsakes which the lady must have given him years ago. But as for harbouring an attachment for a woman he had loved ten years prior, it was not to be understood quickly. Perhaps Cathy was mistaken, and she hoped most fervently that it was so, but there could be no other explanation for now.

However, she had not long to deliberate these questions, for now a disturbance on the stair above her made her shrink once again into the alcove in the hallway, and moments later a shadowy figure, this time carrying no candle at all, slipped past her in the semi-darkness. The figure, of course, was familiar to her. It was none other than Captain Frederick Tilney! And he was carrying a small, dark bundle.

Having now been more astonished than she had ever been in her life, Catherine was now almost overcome when Captain Tilney paused outside the cellar door, tried it, and upon finding it unlocked disappeared into its darkness. Catherine was transfixed. What in heaven's name was going on at Woodston? Three visits to the cellar on the same evening, each person likely unaware of the other — what on earth did it all mean?

She waited, shivering, for the night had grown cold even with her shawl. A few minutes later, Captain Tilney, too, furtively re-entered the hallway and quietly closed the cellar door behind him. No dark package returned with him. His hands were bare. Catherine watched from her hiding place. Captain Tilney did not return upstairs, however, for which she was thankful, for she was sure that if he returned past her he would not fail to discover her there. But to her relief Tilney turned and went toward the kitchen and disappeared in the gloom.

Wondering if the General, too, was to come downstairs to carry out some business in the cellar, Catherine waited some further minutes before moving. All now seemed quiet and she slipped into the library. A faint light came from the study, but now Catherine did not wish to meet Henry. Instead, she took up a taper and relit her extinguished candle from the fire which still burned dimly in the grate. Creeping from the room, she was now determined to investigate the cellar.

Stealing into the hallway again, she, too, turned the cellar door handle, and leaving the door slightly ajar, crept down those stairs, the fourth person to have done the very same thing that evening. On gaining the large bottle-lined room, she lifted her candle and inspected as much as she could see. To her eye there was no difference to when she was last in the room, and she had almost turned away when her eye came to rest upon a wine glass hidden behind one of the port bottles at about eye level on one of the walls.

Moving closer, she lifted the port bottle to move it aside and discovered that it was only about half full. Picking up the glass which had caught her eye in the candlelight, she sniffed. The distinct smell of port lurked in the glass and she replaced it on the shelf thoughtfully, careful to place the port bottle in front of it again.

Moving into the smaller room she went immediately to the chest, for there was little enough to be seen in the rest of the room. Opening the chest, she gasped. She had not expected the handkerchief and ring to be lying at the bottom of the chest, for these things she knew to have been removed by Henry less than an hour before. But lying at the bottom of the chest in their place was a small parcel, tied up in cloth. This was most certainly, she thought, Captain Tilney's doing. She lifted up the little bundle, and placing her candle on the shelf, she unwrapped the cloth, and her mouth dropped open in silent astonishment. In her hand, nestled in the blue cloth, were two gold necklaces, one with a miniature of a pretty young woman, and one with a cross, and with them were a ring of gold, and a gold bracelet inset with three tiny rubies. She turned over the locket and held it up to the candlelight. Engraved upon the back were the words 'Francis E. Tilney, 1758.'

Sixteen

Catherine lay in bed, her head bursting, and her heart full. Sleep was impossible. Henry had not returned to their room and now she was glad of it, for she did not think she would be able to bear the agony of his lying beside her and thinking of someone else.

Catherine had been able to imagine nothing with any confidence, until this moment. Now, conjecture and surmise had transformed in her mind to solid, material fact. Now, where all had been secrets, mysteries and indecipherable signs, truth and plainness were laid bare before her at last.

It did not take much cleverness to discover Mrs Poulter's secret, for it was plain that for some time she had been drinking Henry's decent port in the privacy of the cellar, and that must explain why the woman had been so reluctant for Catherine to go below, why she frequently kept the cellar locked, and why she had been seen on more than one occasion by Catherine leaving the cellar without an unopened bottle in her hand.

But the discovery of two greater secrets, secrets which she would now give anything to not have been privy to, weighed heavily upon Catherine's mind and heart. She almost rose up again, to go to Eleanor's chamber and confide in the one person she knew would be able to give her guidance, but she stopped herself, fearing to burden Eleanor too. Eleanor must never know the pain which Henry had occasioned Catherine, must not be forced to think of her brother with less affection that she did now. It would be too bad to spoil their perfectly amiable relationship.

And Catherine could not approach Henry, not yet, for perhaps there was some chance that she had misjudged, or that there was some other explanation for Henry's having hidden the handkerchief and ring in the cellar himself, a fact which now seemed obvious. And yet why would he have fetched them out again, if not to look at them— but she could not bear to think of it!

Then her folly of the past came to her mind. Last year, at Northanger, she had been quick to judge, too soon to think ill. Now all seemed hopeless, all lost between her and Henry, but she was too much in misery to think rationally, she told herself. No, she must wait, judging and acting in the future with the greatest circumspection, and perhaps by and by she would know how to proceed.

And the final mystery, of the stolen objects in the cellar, perhaps this weighed upon her mind even more heavily than anything, for it was clear now who had taken the Tilney jewels, who had hidden them away, and tried to pass the crime onto another. What Frederick Tilney was about in placing them at Woodston, Catherine could hardly say, but she knew that she must say something to him, to plead with him with the greatest urgency to replace the items at once and confess to his father. If he did not, Henry might be accused of the theft and this Catherine could not bear. She could not allow it, even if her husband no longer loved her. She determined to go directly to Captain Tilney's chamber, as soon as it was light, and confess what she knew to him and beg him to act with the moral rectitude by which he ought to be guided.

Settling these points within herself, she became at length more tolerably composed, although it was some time after the clock in the downstairs hallway intoned four before she fell at last into restless slumber.

When she awoke, Henry had been and gone, leaving only his linen shirt and some used water in the wash basin. It stung her heart that he must think so badly of her that he would not kiss her awake as he was used to doing. To her heart, it was further proof that his affections were no longer her own. And yet she would not retract her accusation against Mrs Poulter, for now she knew the woman to be availing herself of Henry's cellar, Catherine could not begin to guess what other marks upon the housekeeper's character she might discover. Now it was even more conceivable that the woman might have salted her soup, in order to discredit Catherine in Henry's eyes.

Catherine helped herself into her dark blue long-sleeved muslin gown, tying the laces and strings herself, and put her hair up hastily, with no regard for style. Throwing a warm wrap about her shoulders, she left the room and went immediately to Captain Tilney's door. Knocking, she waited, her heart pounding, but when the door opened and a half-dressed Frederick Tilney stood on the threshold with his mocking smile, she lifted her chin. 'Captain Tilney. Forgive me for disturbing you, but I must speak to you directly on a matter most urgent.'

'Must you indeed!' He eyed her lazily. 'Then you had better come in.'

Tilney, his dark hair tousled, and his shirt only half tucked into his pantaloons, looked almost boyish, she thought. Hardly the thief she had come to accuse him of being! She stepped through the door as he waved her in and took the seat to which his movements inclined her.

Leaving the door open, Tilney remained standing where he was. 'To what do I owe the unexpected pleasure of so early a visit?'

Her voice was low, but urgent. 'I shall not do you the dishonour, Sir, of dissembling; I know what you have hidden in my husband's wine cellar, and I desire you should remove them at once, and make a full confession to your father before Henry is blamed.'

Tilney had blanched a little but had recovered at once. He now closed the door hastily. 'Ah! You do, do you?' he replied, his lips curling upward, although Catherine could not tell if it was in amusement or anger.

'I do, indeed! I am shocked, Captain Tilney, but I saw you, you know — I saw with my own eyes, that you entered the cellar late last night. I— I happened to be — in the hallway —' she faltered, suddenly embarrassed to be admitting that she had spied upon him.

It was enough, however. Tilney's countenance had become stony. 'And from this circumstance, you imply that I have hidden some sort of stolen loot here?'

"*Captain Tilney. I must speak with you directly on a matter most urgent.*"

'No, indeed,' cried a vexed Catherine, 'I do not imply it, I *know* it to be true! It was *you* who stole your mother's jewels — pray don't think me so innocent, Captain, that I cannot put facts together and come to a rational conclusion! If you try to deny it I will —'

'You will do what, Mrs Tilney? Tell my father?' Tilney interjected grimly. 'If you tell my father, it will be all over between me and him, and most likely between me and Miss Sweeting, too. You would not do that to my father, I think. He is expecting my union to the wealthy Miss Sweeting to carry away several debts he owes on Northanger; besides, he would be very unhappy to learn the truth about my mother's jewels.'

Catherine was pale but remained firm. 'If you will not confess it, Sir, then you leave me no choice but to inform Henry, and *he* will soon tell your father, I believe! I cannot understand why you brought them here, but I know they are your mother's things; and are you not ashamed to own the theft of your own mother's keepsakes, intended for *your* bride, and offend your mother's memory to such an astonishing degree? I cannot account for it at all!'

Tilney laughed bitterly. 'Ah Miss Moreland, you are yet the innocent, for all that you have been married three months! Your tender sensibilities, no doubt, are offended, just as you were offended last year in the pump rooms when your friend Miss Thorpe and I indulged ourselves in a little... conversation... but I see you have still not forgiven me on that score. Oh, pray don't take the trouble to comment — it is long forgotten with me, I assure you. No, you wish to know why I have been forced into a situation where I have been obliged to borrow my mother's things until such a time as I can reclaim them? I shall tell you.'

'Do,' cried Catherine, 'do indeed, and I hope very much it is a story which has something in it to excuse you for what you have done!'

'Very well. In short, Mrs Tilney,' he began, 'I happened to owe a gentleman acquaintance of mine some money, from a game of cards; I happened to lose rather a large sum, and lately the man has been harassing me to pay up. I have assured him that all will be paid back in good time, when I marry, but the gentleman has insisted upon immediate payment. I was obliged to take my mother's things — half of which are my own right, I remind you — borrowing Henry's portion also, with the intention of exchanging them for blunt in town. I sent my boy off to do the job, with the intention of claiming the items back once I had married Miss Sweeting. Damned things were refused where I had had them taken, however, since it became known that the goods were missing. Chap at the shop where I took them had already been on the lookout, and being a strictly honest fellow, he warned Price, my errand boy, not to show 'em in town again. He claimed he knew to whom they belonged and would inform every pawn shop in the county. My father has already been given the intelligence that the items were presented at an establishment in town and has sent a man in to investigate.

'So you see I have had my hands tied, since now I cannot pawn them at all. I'm in rather a predicament, as you must see. I cannot return them openly, since Father will at once guess how it is, and so I resolved to store them here at Woodston until I could have a servant put them back, perhaps in a drawer or cupboard, and pretend that they were overlooked in the first search. I must rely upon your discretion, Mrs Tilney, to allow me time to see the items returned.'

Catherine had heard all this with growing incredulity. 'But if you return the jewellery, Sir, what will happen? Will your friend be satisfied that you will repay him after you are married to Miss Sweeting? And it is very shocking, very shocking indeed, to think poor Miss Sweeting will have to pay your gambling debts!'

'I hardly know how to answer you. I cannot return the jewellery myself — I have already asked Eleanor to do it but my sister is too much like you, Miss Moreland, and is possessed of too excellent a character to allow her to deceive my father.' His tone was amused.

'Of course!' interrupted Catherine, ignoring his sardonic use of her name, '*that* is what you were arguing about last night! But how did Eleanor guess it was you who had taken the jewels? I cannot imagine you confessing to such an act!'

Tilney laughed bitterly again. 'My sister knows me too well and guessed my secret recently. She is too good for me, I am afraid. She has had the sense to loan me the sum needed to pay off my associate, rather than see my body carried off in a coffin.'

Then you are most fortunate to have such a sister!' cried Catherine angrily. 'But I have a notion that Eleanor would be urging you to confess to your father and hope not too much damage is done! It is the only right thing to do, I am sure!'

'My dear sister has urged me upon the same course as you have suggested, but if I confess to father, then it will be all over with Miss Sweeting, and I cannot have it. She is an amiable girl, naive, certainly, but that is just what I like in a wife, for I must dispose of a tolerable sum after our marriage to discharge my debt, and she will not miss it. If she does, she will not mind, for I am sure she would rather have a living husband than a dead one! The union *must* go ahead!'

Catherine's face was pale. She rose from her chair. 'And this is why you were so ready to join your father in a visit here, after Henry had said you never come to Woodston, and claimed it was dull! And here I thought you a reformed person! Can you sleep easily, Captain, being the author of so much untruth and stratagem? I could not!'

'But you are a prim little girl, Miss Morland, just out of apron-strings, for all that you are a married lady. Your innocence is charming but it leads you to think too well of others, and attribute motives which I own are too good for *me*, at any rate.' He was laughing at her, but his eyes were cold.

'Stop calling me Miss Morland!' cried Catherine, vexed. 'I am not a child any longer! Whatever you think of me, Captain, I am resolved not to change my course. You must return the jewels, and risk hurting your father and your chance of matrimony. If Eleanor does not tell your father, I will certainly tell Henry, if you do not! I cannot be a party to dishonesty, and I only hope you will see how excessively wicked and evil it would be to carry on as you have planned. Good morning, Captain Tilney.'

Catherine left the room, her head and heart in turmoil. Eleanor had *known* of this! — it must be what she had hinted at, when she had said she wished to see Captain Tilney. Catherine was heartened by the thought and found ease and comfort in knowing herself not the only person to be party to such a secret. Eleanor must be determined upon a right course of action, and Catherine would by and by consult her and tell her that she, too, had urged Captain Tilney to confess. And if Miss Sweeting chose to give up the union when she found out what kind of man her husband was, she could certainly not be blamed for such a course!

Going directly to Eleanor's room, she knocked, and was admitted at once. Eleanor had been up and dressed for some time, being unable to sleep, she said. Upon finding Catherine knew that Captain Tilney had been the one who had taken Mrs Tilney's jewels, Eleanor was astonished. 'But how came you to discover Frederick's involvement in this scandal?' she asked in some consternation.

Without saying anything about Henry's movements the previous evening, Catherine quickly related all she had seen last night of Captain Tilney entering the cellar, and her own further investigation of the chest in the interior room. She completed the tale with a recounting of her visit to Captain Tilney's room from where she had just come. 'But I cannot say, Eleanor, if your brother was much persuaded by my words; I only hope he confesses to your father. I feel that I ought to tell Henry. What do you think of the scheme? What is your advice?'

Eleanor was busy fitting a lace cap over her curls, but she turned from the glass to Catherine. She sighed. 'I fear for my brother, Catherine. I knew of his habit, and in truth, I have been obliged before to loan him money over it, but this, this is beyond what I could have anticipated. I can hardly say if he will confess to Father. But it is the only course of action. He must see that!'

'I think if he does not confess this morning, you must tell your father. I would be very sorry to prevent his marrying Miss Sweeting, but it is very wicked that he wishes to use her money to pay his gambling debts!'

Eleanor smiled her gentle smile. 'You are sweetly innocent, Catherine, and I love you the more for it, but Frederick does not care in the way you and I do, about things we call "wicked". He cares only for himself, I am afraid. But I mean to tell Henry, since it is partly his share of my mother's things too. After all, it is my mother's memory my brother has defiled, and as much as I want to protect Frederick, I owe the truth to my father.'

These words heartened Catherine, and after a moment more they went downstairs together to breakfast, Catherine much relieved to share the burden of at least one of her secrets!

Seventeen

In due course, that morning both Captain Tilney and Eleanor went to Henry in his study and were some time in conversation there.

Eleanor emerged sometime later and told Catherine all that had transpired. 'My brother was contrite, and I do believe he regrets his actions, Catherine. Henry has extracted a promise from Frederick to inform our father of his part in the disappearance of my mother's things, but he will wait until they are home at Northanger. This way, it will not create a disturbance while we are guests here. It is the only way, I think,' she added sadly. 'Frederick has returned to Henry the necklace and bracelet which my mother intended for his bride; I am sure you will be in possession of them soon enough, as you deserve. As for Frederick, he has promised that he will not attempt to dispose of the other items, but will give them as intended to Miss Sweeting if she consents to the marriage after these events are revealed.'

'And I suppose they must be exposed, eventually, must not they? It would be very wicked for Captain Tilney to deceive Miss Sweeting now; but do you think the lady will wish to marry someone with such large debts? I am afraid I hardly know what is proper in these circumstances,' added Catherine doubtfully.

Eleanor shook her head. 'I hardly know myself. Perhaps Miss Sweeting will not marry my brother, unless she is very much in love with him, but in that case, I feel all the more pity for her! But we must not forget that she has her own fortune and can afford to be as particular as she wishes.'

'I do hope she is not so *very* much in love with your brother, for then she may suffer greatly.'

'I only hope that his actions do not injure her reputation, for that would be a graver injury indeed!'

They spent the day quietly, avoiding Captain Tilney, and Catherine was grateful that Henry had gone out early with the General to go over the estate. By the time they had returned for dinner, Henry had recovered his good spirits, and although he was slightly cool toward his brother for the remainder of their time at Woodston, he was not so ungenerous as to spite him with looks or words. Catherine knew that the General would not take the news of his son's betrayal so well as Henry had, however, and could not but help feel a little pity for Captain Tilney, when she contemplated the possibility of his losing his father's favour, as well as that of his betrothed.

As for Henry, all seemed returned to normal. He had kissed Catherine with as much affection as he always did when he had finally seen her at dinner, and although nothing could be said on the topic of the soup, Catherine's mind was put somewhat to rest over their disagreement with the return of his good humour. It was difficult, however, to be unrestrained with him, for she knew that very likely, he was suffering a great deal in knowing himself to be married to one, when attached to another! She suffered very much when she allowed her mind to dwell on her circumstance, and doubt ravaged her peace each time he spoke kindly to her. Surely he could not behave with his usual natural ease if he was in love with another? But there could be no other explanation for the things she had seen the previous night. Perhaps she was, after all, entirely mislead on the matter, but she could not see another way through it all, although she tried in vain.

She was careful to speak nothing but what was uncontentious, amiable, nothing calculated to stir his disgust at her doubting of Mrs Poulter's good motives. He did not refer again to their conversation of the previous evening and she did not bring it to his notice. She was quieter than usual for the following two days, which he seemed not to notice, for his own preoccupation had prevented him from hearing her speak on several occasions; indeed, he seemed to Catherine to be quite distracted and occasionally even was cool towards her, which in turn made her ever more miserable, knowing what — *who* — it must be that occupied his mind. It preyed upon her thoughts, oppressing her even by day, so that she, too, became ever more distracted and cool in turn.

The General and Captain Tilney drove away in their carriage one cold morning three days after they had arrived, and Eleanor left them shortly afterwards.

'I shall write my father as soon as I return home,' she told Catherine. 'I suspect Frederick will tell Father directly, for he would not wish the news to come from me, I collect, but I shall write nonetheless, and offer my strongest urgings to my father not to cast Frederick off.'

'Perhaps your father will be lenient, seeing as Captain Tilney is the oldest son. He cannot prevent him from inheriting Northanger, after all!'

Eleanor smiled warmly. 'You are too good, too liberal, too generous a creature, Catherine! My brother has chosen a pearl among women, indeed, to be his wife!'

Catherine could make no reply to this, and instead, hiding her misery as best she could, embraced her sister-in-law and bid her visit again as soon as she could be spared from her husband.

~ ~ * ~ ~

Four weeks passed by, then five, and soon it was February. Catherine had now begun to doubt her own surmisings as to Henry's affections being engaged elsewhere, for all normality had returned to Woodston, and Henry was as attentive and kind as he had ever been. Perhaps Catherine had been mistaken, after all? She had almost given up the idea, with great relief, that Henry was still in love with this Miss Parkhurst. Still, questions filled her mind when it was not occupied with other matters and her nights gave her restless, disturbed sleep.

They had received no letter from the General, nor from Eleanor, and the date of Captain Tilney's marriage had passed by with no letter confirming the union had taken place. Shortly after this, however, a piece of news arrived at Woodston. Henry had received a letter from his father, confirming that the union which had been expected between his son and Miss Sweeting had not taken place. Despite the contemptuous tone of his language, it seemed that the General had been more lenient than Captain Tilney had deserved, and had forgiven his son, even if he had not borne very gracefully the loss of such a prize as he had speculated upon. Northanger, it seemed, would have to want longer for new-furnishing.

However, as much as the General had found it in his heart to forgive Frederick, it seemed that Miss Sweeting had not. The engagement had been at once broken off, the young lady's father insisting it must be looked upon as a fortunate near miss for his daughter of a union boding such ill-luck, such unhappiness as he could not have allowed. Poor Miss Sweeting had taken her fortune and swept from Frederick's life.

Henry was circumspect about this news, for indeed it was nothing that they had not imagined to be the case. 'Frederick is vastly fortunate that my father has seen fit to forgive him, however,' he added.

'Yes,' replied Catherine, 'I think it must be owing to your sister's intervention, for I believe she must have pleaded very mightily to your father and put such a good account of your brother to him that he could not but act with lenience.'

'As usual, you are too good, Catherine. You believe others capable only of how you yourself would think and act.'

'Then to what do you attribute your father's lenience, if not his good nature, and a perfectly natural love for his son?'

'Perhaps it is as you say, but I know my father, Catherine, and he cannot afford Northanger if Frederick does not marry well. He will now be on the lookout for a new prospect, as Northanger must have its share of Frederick's good fortune.'

'A new prospect! So soon after your brother's broken engagement? How could you say such a thing, Henry?' She sighed. 'But I suppose this is the way of important families; the sons must have something to live on, and marriage is less of a convenience than a necessity.'

'Indeed. For Fred, at least, it must be so. I wager that my freedom-loving brother will be married within a twelve-month, and to some lady of more than common fortune! But I confess I own myself as cynical as ever; it appears to me that poor Miss Sweeting has had a lucky reprieve!'

After this, Catherine did not any more doubt the truth of her husband's surmises over his brother, but they did not have to wait a twelve-month to hear of Frederick's fate. Only a week after they had heard of the broken engagement, a second, even more astonishing piece of news made its way to Woodston.

Catherine received a letter from Eleanor, with the most incredible news. Captain Tilney, it seemed, being cast off by one heiress, had soon found another — in the form of none other than Miss Isabella Thorpe! A hasty marriage had taken place, and the new-married couple were expected at Torrington House in very short time, and from there, they would go to Northanger to settle.

Catherine was all incredulity united with no trifling amount of horror. 'I can hardly believe it!' she cried, thrusting the letter at Henry. 'Can it be true? Isabella! The most contemptible, cunning flirt — to marry your brother after all!' She did not add that she thought the pair quite fit for one another, for she did not wish to occasion Henry pain by injuring his family loyalties, but she was more bitter over the match than she would have Henry guess at.

Henry was circumspect. 'I am a little astonished, I confess, but not so very much, Catherine. As much as you know what Miss Thorpe is, I know full well what my brother is and what his motivations must be. Her fortune has made her eligible, and he does not scruple to be particular regarding from where the fortune comes, so long as he marries one. Carry on, do finish reading the letter!'

It was, Eleanor had written warmly, her greatest anxiety that the news should come from herself, before Catherine heard of it through any other channel. She was sensible of its being a most delicate and sensitive matter, considering Catherine's brother's disappointment at the lady's hand last year, and she wished to give Catherine her most heartfelt sympathies, and exhorted her to bear it as "patience on a monument", although she knew it would not be borne easily.

Henry was not as sympathetic. 'I see what you are feeling, but my sister is right — you must bear up under the pain of knowing what she was to your brother, as best you can.'

'Yes, but it is all so— so— vexing! I cannot say the fortune is all on her side, for I collect it must be seen as equal, since he will benefit from her money, and she from his connections; but to think of it — your brother and Miss Thorpe! But perhaps she may be happy, now that she has got the man she wanted, and a fortune besides!'

'If,' remarked Henry with a short laugh, 'he does not spend it all; perhaps they will be happy together. I hope that my father, at least, will be content with such a daughter-in-law. She does bring to Northanger a much looked-for bounty.'

Catherine contented herself with the thought that perhaps Isabella, in marrying Captain Tilney, would suffer as just a punishment as was merited, and she could not help feeling most offended on account of her brother. After treating her brother with the contempt with which she had cast him off, it seemed unfair for Isabella to have inherited a fortune and then gained the very man for whom she had thrown James over, but it seemed that there was no accounting for the way providence worked. James must hear of it too, and it pained Catherine that her brother would likely be ever more grieved by the whole affair.

Her own troubles haunted Catherine too, and as each day passed she could do little but try to preserve that small peace which routine and sameness confer. She could not account for what she had seen the night of the dinner without suspecting Henry of his being in love with someone else, and yet his attentions to herself seemed genuine. Sometimes she even thought that there must be some other explanation for his behaviour, and for the items he had removed from the cellar. But she dared not ask, and as the days passed, it grew more difficult, and more unthinkable, to approach him.

And then there was the matter of the returned jewels. By now, Catherine had expected Henry to present her with the things Mrs Tilney had left for her, as Henry's wife. But nothing had been given her and he had not so much as mentioned the topic. She thought with misery of his desiring to give them to another, and when weeks had passed with no mention of the gold ring and bracelet, it seemed to confirm even more all that Catherine suspected.

Eighteen

One cold day in late February, Henry was as usual absent from home on parish duties, and for once Catherine was glad to be alone. It was increasingly difficult to bear being in the same room, to receive his smiles and attentiveness. On the surface these appeared to her as not to have changed, but she had now often observed him in private, and her observations told her that he seemed an altered creature. In essentials, he was much the same, jovial and pleasant, but on those occasions where he felt himself concealed by privacy of solitude, she saw that he was increasingly troubled, and a frown often overspread his countenance.

Upon Henry's return that afternoon he kissed her distractedly, then took up his mail as was his custom. Seizing upon a letter which had arrived from town, he at once betook himself into his study without so much as an apology to Catherine.

Emerging shortly afterward, he rang for Mrs Poulter and turned to Catherine. 'I am heartily sorry for it, Catherine, but I have been called away to town on important business. I hope,' he added with a short laugh, 'that you will this time refrain from laundering my cravats, dearest.'

Catherine detected in Henry's tone a coolness which had never been present before, and it cut her to the heart. *She* could not find amusement in the little stab at her foolish scrapes, even if he could. With a heavy heart, she wondered if it was Miss Parkhurst whom he was going to see, but then checked herself.

Henry would never betray her to that extent, she was sure, but still, his going away was not news which gave her any pleasure.

Mrs Poulter entered the room at this moment, and Catherine heard him order up his carriage. When the housekeeper had gone to do as bid, Catherine went to Henry and softly laid her head upon his heart. 'Must you go?'

He kissed her head a moment but was unmoved. 'Aye, I have urgent business in town, and it will not wait. I am eager to get done with it — never mind, but I shall expect you to bear my absence with less trouble than did you last time I was gone away.' His eyes were stern.

'When shall you return?' She spoke quietly and gave no hint of the turmoil which was passing through her mind.

'I shall not be away many days. Perhaps three or four, if I take the match-bays, and travel at pace. They can manage the distance better than the chestnut mare, I collect. At any rate, I shall post up to town this very hour. And Catherine, when I return, we must have a serious talk.'

Catherine, finding his manner to be uncommonly serious for the light-hearted Henry that she was accustomed to, shivered at this. What could he have to say to her, but to confess his love for another woman, or perhaps to scold her for having humiliated him in front of his family, or both, even! She could hardly lift her eyes to his when he met her a half hour later, dressed in his great coat.

'I — I will not like to be without you.' Her eyes watered.

'Nor I, but it cannot be helped. I will explain all when I return.'

'Henry? There is something I must talk to you about. I — I can hardly —'

Henry was growing impatient. 'Whatever it is, can it not wait, Catherine? Forgive me, but I am eager to make town by tonight.' He entered the carriage and turned back to her, making at attempt at humour. 'I shall not be many days, my dear. But if I am later than four, come find me, for I am sure to have fallen sacrifice to the arts of some fat innkeeper who will no doubt make me drunk and keep me prisoner in the barn. I shall rely on you!'

Not seeing the wetness on her cheeks, he kissed her briefly and knocked sharply on the roof for the driver to get up the horses and Catherine watched the carriage roll at a good pace up the drive and out the gates.

~ ~ * ~ ~

A day passed, and the following morning found Catherine wandering the downstairs hall once again. She entered the library where Mrs Poulter had had Emily make up a good fire, for the weather was cold and snow threatened, although it did not make good just yet on its greying, ominous looks.

She spent an hour looking over the novels and histories on the shelves, and wondered if she had better not practice her pianoforte, or take up her painting things, but the painting master not being due until the afternoon, she could not raise any urgency to paint, although she liked in general to dab away at her paper. Feeling no great desire to do anything at all, she left the library and went into Henry's study. She sat in his chair, remembering their first month of marriage, and the delight she had taken in feeling herself treasured and loved by such a man as her husband. What had gone awry? Had she been granted any wish at that moment, if some oriental-looking genie had mysterious appeared before her and granted her heart's desire, she would have wished herself returned to that former time. But alas, she repined, such things as genies remained in books, and were the stuff of fairy tales only.

She absently shifted the papers on his desk, and some words in strong black ink caught her eye. Pulling the letter forward, she began to read, with growing bewilderment and alarm.

Simpson and Harvey Solicitors
Windsor Street
London

Dated this 21ˢᵗ day of February, 1799

Mr Henry Tilney,
In regards, Sir, to the matter discussed with my partner and myself some weeks ago, I am pleased to be able to inform you that the matter has been settled as per your instructions.

The annulment of your marriage may be finalized by the inscribing of your signature on the documents which have been drawn up and held here, at which time you may consider yourself legally released from all obligations to Mrs Tilney.

Kindly appear at our offices at your earliest convenience to settle this matter.

I remain your servant,

J.D. Simspon, (Attorney at Law)

Aghast with horror, Catherine reread the letter but she found it had nothing more to yield but the misery it had already afforded her. She gave a short exclamation of sorrow. There was nothing left to wonder at, nothing to excuse Henry upon, nothing to surmise as she lay in bed at night trying to sleep. Nay, all had now been revealed, all secrets finally opened to her; Henry's object in going to town twice, in great secrecy, was now made quite clear. There was no mistake to be made, no 'perhaps' or 'possibly' to rest upon. No comfort for her feelings would ever be hers. Henry had sought, and at this moment was actively bringing about, the annulment of their marriage, and she must bear the misery and the shame of it!

It was her own fault. He had become disgusted with her, with the shame she had wrought upon him as a clergyman, with a very silly wife, who could not even do laundry, who could not feed fowls without losing them, who could not accompany him charmingly on the pianoforte, and who was incapable of entertaining even a few guests without serving oversalted soup! She had failed him miserably, and now she was seeing the consequences of a foolishly selfish life.

But how could he do such a thing without informing her, without giving her a chance to beg his forgiveness? She supposed she had been very wicked, or at least very foolish, but still — to annul their marriage? Resentment worked its way into her heart and the words Mr Longstaff had uttered to her now came to her mind. It really was very wrong of Henry to have left her, as if he did not care for her, and go out for so many hours, on so many days! She was expected to shift for herself, to find her way as the new mistress of Woodston, with only a resentful housekeeper for company. Perhaps Mr Longstaff was right and Henry had not cared for her as he ought? Was it entirely her own fault that she had gotten herself into so many scrapes?

Anger and misery raged alternately in her breast, and for a time she was powerless to move. Then, after about half an hour's free indulgence in grief, resentment, and self-pity, she took herself into the garden, there to wander aimlessly, grieving for her lost husband. Now she need not wonder what Henry had wished to talk to her about when he returned, for it was clear he would then break the news to her, and, she supposed, request her to pack her things and return to Fullerton.

The air was crisp, but the sun was out and gave her a little warmth as she wandered along the winding path which led down to the stream. She picked wildflowers as she walked, gathering them in her hand. It gave her a small comfort to do so, saying their names under her breath. 'Bellis perennis. Ranunculus. Hyacinthoides.'

Eleanor's little botany book had, after all, been of some use to her, she thought with bitterness, for the utterances of the names of the flowers calmed her somewhat. Allowing the activity to occupy her mind, she was able to drive her encroaching wretchedness away just a little. After she had gathered a colourful profusion of wild blooms in her hands, she took them to the seat next to the little bridge which crossed the stream, where she sat limply, wondering what she ought to do next. Should she go to Fullerton, perhaps, before Henry came home? Or wait to confront him?

Never had Catherine more wanted a cordial, a tonic for her nerves, a balm for her breaking heart. Henry, who was her own dear Henry, who for all his high principles, his seeming constancy, wished their marriage annulled. On what grounds he could have it done, she had no notion; she had never paid attention to dull legal matters, and her father had only ever married people himself — she had nothing on which to judge her position.

On whatever grounds Henry might find for an annulment, it was bad enough that he desired one. She had almost made up her mind to go directly into the house and begin packing, when Mr Charles Longstaff came around the garden hedge, and perceived her in the distance.

He came towards her and she quickly dried her eyes. But it was not soon enough.

'Are you quite alone again, Mrs Tilney?' He gave her a most speaking look of compassion and regard. 'It pains me to see you so unhappy, if you will forgive my impertinence in saying so. Is there anything I can get you for your relief?' He seated himself quite close to her side.

'Mr Longstaff!' She moved a little to allow for his wishing to share the bench with her, and laughed mirthlessly. 'It is becoming quite a habit with me to be late for my lessons!'

'And to be found weeping in the garden, also, I might add!'

Catherine smiled weakly. 'I cannot deny it, Sir! But as you see, I am not well, and perhaps, if you would be so kind as to allow, you might be so good as to — to put off the lesson again today...' She faltered, holding back tears. Whether she ought to make her distress known to him, she could not judge, so confused she was in her heart and mind. To expose Henry she could not allow, even though she found much wrong in his behaviour. And although she was so burdened under the heavy guilt brought upon her by her own behaviour, she could hardly bear to reveal her shame in front of an acquaintance. She straightened her back and wiped at a lone tear which had found its way down her cheek.

Now Mr Longstaff's arm was about her shoulders, and he was offering her his handkerchief. 'There, there, Mrs Tilney, it cannot possibly be as bad as all that! Perhaps I can call for some salts, or a vinaigrette? You ladies always have these things about you, do you not? Or Mrs Poulter might —'

'Oh, pray, don't trouble Mrs Poulter, please!' cried Catherine so earnestly that Longstaff gave her a very keen look indeed.

'No indeed, I shall not, if it gives you so much anxiety! But will you not confide in me, as a friend? I may be able to advise you, if you will trust me with your confidence?'

Catherine, overwrought and yearning for release, was not able to resist such a kindness, and gave way to tears. She said in a half-articulate jumble of words, 'Oh, it is all a horrid mess, and it is my own fault, and Henry has been in love with another lady all this time and never told me, and now he is so disgusted with me that he wishes our marriage annulled and I hardly know what to do!'

'Good god!' exclaimed Longstaff. 'Are you certain? It seems a very unlikely course, even if I do say so myself, Mrs Tilney. How can you be so sure of its being true? What an evil, what a very evil outcome! And yet, men will be men, you know!'

'Oh but it *is* true, or at least I think it very likely! I saw the letter myself, speaking of the annulment, and Henry has posted up to London only yesterday, to sign the papers, and he has her ring, and a handkerchief, and a lock of her hair too, and everything is so dreadful I can hardly bear it!' She accomplished this outpouring with more tears and sobbed deeply into the borrowed kerchief.

With a gleam in his eye which was entirely lost to Catherine, Longstaff patted her shoulder for a moment or two until she had recovered herself enough to raise red eyes to his. 'Forgive me, Mr Longstaff. I am much better now, I assure you. I am probably mistaken about it all. Henry is truly an excellent husband, and it really is all my own fault if he despises me!'

'Never mind, my dear, I am sure you have done nothing so wicked as to deserve such a punishment, and really if Mr Tilney is displeased with you, it is certainly his own fault for neglecting you so abominably in the first instance. Now, look at me and give me a smile, won't you?' He lifted her chin with his finger, and she raised her eyes obediently.

At this moment, Longstaff leaned in and took the great liberty of putting his lips close to hers as if to kiss her. Catherine watched in morbid fascination as his face drew close, and as if in a dream, she marvelled at why she had not sooner perceived Mr Longstaff's motives. She tried to move, but found she was frozen in place, and could not move a limb if she tried!

Nineteen

If there had been no sufficient principle on either side, this wicked temptation might have run its course, and ended in ever more misery for Catherine. But, although the one party might have had deficiency enough of character to create a chaos from which Catherine and Henry may never have recovered, there was more than enough sufficiency of principle on the other side. Catherine, abruptly finding herself able to move again, shrunk back from the devious drawing instructor.

'What in heaven's name are you doing, Mr Longstaff?' she exclaimed, amazement for the moment making her forget her present unhappiness.

'Only what you have been begging from me since we met,' replied the rapscallion. 'I see you are going to be missish and pretend nothing further could have been from your mind, or some such thing. But I only wanted a little kiss, and you desired me to kiss you.'

'I?' cried Catherine. 'I desired nothing of the sort! How can you have misread anything I have said or done! How could you think of such wickedness when I am already in despair! Am I not wretched enough already? Would you destroy what is left of my pride, Sir?'

'Come now, Mrs Tilney, it was merely a little flirtation, something to divert you from your present troubles!'

'Wicked man! I am a married woman, Mr Longstaff, for all that my husband might have left me forever!'

'Married? But what does that signify to you females, when your husbands are not present? Now, if you were to put aside your very female, your very *fetching* female pride, Mrs Tilney, and consult only your own inclination, would you not rather have a pleasant little interlude every week or so, since you are so much alone here? Your husband need not discover it if *you* do not tell him! Come now — don't be missish and prim!'

'Why should you mean to cut up my peace, whatever of it is still left! I am in anguish, in despair, and here you have come to abuse me! You are — you are despicable!' she exclaimed through her tears.

He stood, as if to take his leave. 'You are irrational, Mrs Tilney, and behaving very foolishly! It was only a little kiss — and why should you mind, if your husband does not? Is he here to protect you? He has treated you with disdain, and has, by your assumption, abandoned you for another. Why you should be so upset with me for offering a little comfort, I cannot imagine! I did not think you a tease!'

'You are excessively wicked! Pray go away! Do!' She had no leisure for noting the angry tears which ran down her face, for she was seized with shock and misery. Reaching for the nearest object to her hand, she dashed her posy of wildflowers at him.

'You females are all the same,' laughed Longstaff, sidestepping the flowers neatly. 'One minute you give a chap a vast deal of encouragement, and the next you are all cold and supercilious. It is impossible to determine your thoughts and designs from one moment to the next. Then you treat a little harmless flirtation as the greatest insult in the world, all the while encouraging it. If I had not been chivalrous, and offered to comfort you with a little kiss, you would have been quite offended. Admit it!'

'Admit it! I certainly shall do no such thing! I think you ought to leave, Mr Longstaff, and pray do me the favour of never returning to Woodston!'

Longstaff shrugged, turned, and retreated along the path, leaving Catherine to sit, once again, before her limbs failed her. Of all the evil events to have befallen her, these past two days had supplied more than enough to occasion her pain for a long time to come.

But the shock of Mr Longstaff's approaches to her had shaken her out of her misery. After a few minutes' reflection on her circumstances, she regained a certain equilibrium and began to be tolerably composed. Rising, she returned to the house, and going immediately to the kitchen, she found Mrs Poulter with Cook, drinking tea at the great kitchen table.

'Mrs Poulter? I wish to speak to you on a matter of some importance.'

The woman had turned to eye her with cold, icy blue eyes. 'Certainly, Mrs Tilney. Of what use may I be to you?' Her eyes mocked, but Catherine held her resolve.

'I know,' said Catherine with great feeling, 'that you have been stealing my husband's port, and drinking it in the cellar. I also know you salted my white soup. For these reasons, Mrs Poulter, you are — you are dismissed.'

The woman turned various shades of pink. 'Now, you look here, Mrs Tilney! I don't know what—'

'You are excused from further duties today, Mrs Poulter. You may collect your things and be gone by tomorrow morning. I would be grateful if you would hand me the keys to the cellar and the other rooms, if you please.'

Mrs Poulter exchanged a look with Cook who lifted her plump form from the chair and promptly slunk away to the pantry as fast as such a move could be executed. Mrs Poulter remained seated, however. 'Now, I don't hardly know what makes you think it was me who salted your soup, Ma'am, but if you insist upon saying such things, I demand proof, or you cannot make me go anywhere. What is more, I shall tell the master when he returns, and I am sure he won't like it if you go dismissing his servants that have been in service at Woodston for nigh on ten years!'

Catherine remained unmoved. Summoning a new-found authority, she held out her hand. 'The keys please Mrs Poulter. And do not expect a character, for I will not write one, and nor shall my husband, not for someone who steals, and — and undermines a new mistress.'

After a moment, Mrs Poulter reached into her pockets and retrieved a ring of keys. Handing them to Catherine ungently, that lady remarked sharply, 'Well I never! I didn't mean no harm! But

I have been in service here for too long to be about accepting orders from a chit of a girl with no notion of how to run a house, and me being so good to the master all these years — I have been loyal servant, Ma'am. And what if I did sup a little of the port when I happened to be down in the cellar? I have asked for nothing more, and taken no more than my fair wages, all these years, Ma'am, and I am sure Mr Tilney would not spite me like you have done and deny me what little comfort for my efforts I can take when I find it!'

'All the same, Mrs Poulter, I desire you will pack your things and be gone after breakfast tomorrow. Good day!'

Catherine marched from the kitchen. Having completed the first task she had set herself, she went upstairs to complete the second, final task.

Taking out her writing desk, she penned a short note. It read thus:

> *Dearest Henry,*
>
> *I did not mean to pry, but I confess I have discovered the letter from London. I cannot write how much pain it gives me to know that I have disappointed you. You must be disgusted with me, and I can hardly blame you. I understand what must be done. To imagine you thinking ill of me is more than I can bear, even while we stay in this house together. I shall return to Fullerton. I can only beg your forgiveness, and that you will by and by not think so ill of me as you do presently.*
>
> *Believe me to be your most sincerely afflicted, and deeply ashamed*
>
> *Catherine*

Three hours later, she had managed to pack her trunks, place her hats neatly into their hat boxes, and had put out her travelling jacket and bonnet, ready to put on in the morning.

Now, her things packed, and her temper, her emotions, her misery contained strictly within the confines of her breaking heart, she sat cool and unmoving in the light of her window upon the bed which she had shared for four months with her husband. Its white covering was soft under her hand and she leaned back upon the pillows, trying very hard not to cry yet more tears.

It would be so relieving to go home to Fullerton, to be once again among her friends, to feel herself cherished by those who had known her all her life. She had failed at being a wife, but she might yet redeem herself as a daughter and sister to those whom she loved best, apart from Henry and Eleanor.

That her husband did not love her was plain, and she augured nothing but further misery if she remained to hear him out when he returned. She knew her follies, her shortcomings, and her undisciplined ways. To think all these months she had been so set upon making herself into an accomplished lady, playing games with herself, playing at being a wife, when all the while she had failed to develop the truly important qualities of self-discipline, studiousness, and courage. She had sought to become a better housewife, but had failed by letting Mrs Poulter intimidate her. She had played at being a wife to Henry, rather than truly making the role her own.

And now Henry despised her so much that another woman had taken her place in his heart! It was not to be born, and yet it must. She would go to Fullerton and learn to be a better person. No more would she play at being a fine lady, learning pianoforte when she hated the instrument, drawing and painting to please another, reading history to make Henry happy, when she had never made herself happy by it! This time she would watch her mother and learn truly how to be a useful sort of person, rather than setting store in being an accomplished one! How foolish she had been! No wonder Henry reviled and despised her!

A lonely tear dripped down her cheek, but she would not let herself cry. She folded herself into the warmth of the coverlet, and by and by she fell into a dark, dreamless sleep.

Twenty

Fullerton was as warm, busy and welcoming as Woodston had become empty and cold. Catherine had not confessed the reason for her visit home, but as she sat in the drawing room with her mother and younger sisters, sipping tea, she was hard put to quell the tears which rose up in her eyes and threatened to spill over her pale cheeks. Sarah, her sister, was full of hovering attendance and sweet attentiveness, but this kindness was more a bane than a balm to Catherine's nerves, since it made her think constantly of Woodston, and the attentiveness which had marked her first month with Henry — the same attentiveness which had been so markedly absent in the last.

Mrs Moreland, observing her daughter's pale drawn looks, was wise and said little this first day but to welcome Catherine and assure her that she might stay just as long as she liked, until Henry fetched her home again. 'You should not like to be away from Henry for too long, I am sure,' she said cheerfully. 'But we are very glad to have you here even if only for a week or two!'

To this Catherine could not reply, for she did not know that she would ever show her face at Woodston again! To this end, she knew that she must write to Henry. She had left him that cold little note, telling him where she had gone to, but it had been hard enough to write that much, and she did not, just yet, feel equal to a longer letter. She would, in due course, perhaps in a few days, feel strong enough to write him more fully.

What would he think, when he returned from London to find her gone? What would he think when he found her note to him? Would he be glad to know the awkward business of asking her to pack her things and leave Woodston was taken care of already? He would, she was sure, be very angry with her for dismissing Mrs Poulter, and Mr Longstaff too, but if he knew what anguish both had caused her, he would understand, she was sure. Still, Mrs Poulter had been in his employ for ten years and she feared his anger although she did not regret dismissing the woman.

What would he think when he found Mr Longstaff had been sent home, too? But he would not know what had taken place, and if he did, perhaps he would even blame her. If he knew the truth, would he perhaps come to his senses and come after her to beg her to return? But how could he, when it seemed so very likely, almost certain, that he was still in love with Miss Parkhurst. It was not possible, she thought, and shook her head with a heavy sigh, which did not go unnoticed by her mother.

'George, Harriet,' Mrs Moreland commanded after a little while, 'do go into the stables and fetch one or two of the kittens — perhaps Catherine would like to hold them, since she has not yet seen them?'

'Oh, yes! Catherine, you simply must see Daisy's kittens! They are so pretty and sweet!' cried little Harriet, who had been dangling onto Catherine's hand since she had sat down.

'Then I must certainly see them,' replied Catherine, trying for a watery smile.

Harriet and George ran off together, and Sarah, who was only two years younger than Catherine, sat close by and took her hand, 'Won't you tell Mama and me what is troubling you, Catherine dear? I can see that you are in low spirits! Surely Henry would not like you to be unhappy if you are come away to have amusement and rest?'

'If you are in some kind of trouble, Catherine, it would be as well to tell me, so your father and I can best know how to act on your behalf,' added her mother anxiously.

With her two younger siblings gone from the room, all restraint was lost, and Catherine gave way to tears, and presently some of her anxieties and doubts were revealed; her failure at housekeeping, the scrapes she had gotten herself into, the unpleasant Mrs Poulter, the sad tale of the ruined cravats and lost hen, the failed soup, and most of all, the conviction that she had lost Henry's respect. Almost all was revealed, but she could not bring herself to utter her deepest conviction that she had lost Henry's love, and that she had been supplanted in his affections by an old *paramour*. This secret she kept in her heart, for it was of all things, perhaps, the most shameful secret of all, and she could not bear to return home and be thought such a failure in the eyes of her family, although she knew it could not long be concealed.

Her mother, always a philosophical, prosaic being, listened quietly to Catherine's tale of woe. 'Perhaps there is less harm done than you suspect, Catherine. You always were sad, shatter-brained creature, but on the whole, my dear, what you have told us sounds not so very bad. Your husband is a good man, the finest-tempered, most amiable fellow. Perhaps you have misjudged him, Catherine? He cannot be so angry with you after all! It has only been four months since you went away to Woodston, and learning to run a household is not easy. Why, when I married your father and became a clergyman's wife, it took me a year to find my feet! Depend upon it, my dear, you have not lost your husband's respect, nor his affections. I would vouchsafe to say that they are as firm as ever they were, if only you would trust them!'

Catherine wanted very much to agree, but ventured doubtfully, 'I wish it were true, Mama, only he has been so cold with me, so distracted, that I hardly know what to think! Oh Mama, I have been the most foolish, sad girl! I ought to have attended you when you offered to show me so many things, and instead I chose to have my head in a book. Then I thought that improving myself meant to paint and draw and learn my instrument, and I tried ever so hard to learn those accomplishments which would make Henry proud of me, but I was so mistaken, so wrong! I was plumped up with foolish pride — ridiculous ideas of improvement — and only recently have I realised that Henry neither wanted nor expected me to be accomplished — he wanted me to learn common sense, and learn practical things, and discipline, and courage! I have so disappointed him! No wonder he is vexed and disgusted with me!'

'There, there,' comforted her sister, taking her hand, 'I am sure it is not as bad as that!'

Mrs Moreland nodded. 'You will give us a few days of your company, Catherine, and learn to be rational and calm again, and by and by I am certain you will feel that you have unjustly accused yourself. Sleep on it, and we will go to call on Mrs Allen tomorrow, and you will be entertained and distracted enough by your brothers and sisters to be content again. There is nothing like distraction to soothe unhappiness!'

Catherine could not bring herself to tell her mother what had happened in the garden, how she had been accosted by Mr Longstaff, and the humiliation and anger she had experienced. But these offences were trifling in comparison with the conviction that she had lost Henry forever, and that she might never see him again! These unhappinesses, she thought, she might never recover from, no matter how many kittens were offered for her distraction!

Catherine spent a sleepless night, her mind going over and over the dreadful events of the last few days. She was still shocked by Mr Longstaff's dreadful actions, but it was the thought of losing, of having most likely already lost, Henry's regard, his love, his tender affections, which kept her from sleep.

She was received the next day with a great deal of kindness by the Allens, for whom she had always had a steady affection, and they for her. Their kindness comforted her, and the remembrance that she had many friends at Fullerton made her more easy, even if she could not be content. But thoughts of Henry returning home about now, and finding her gone, plagued her even so.

She spent the rest of the day entertaining her little brothers and sisters, helping them with their reading and writing, and assisting her mother in milking the cow and feeing the hens. 'I have been so foolish,' she confided, as she scattered corn and watched as the hens ran to gobble it up. 'Now I am eager to improve myself, not for fine living, but for practical living; things which would have made Henry proud of me. I did not even know how to feed the hens, then!'

Her mother shook her head. 'You have learned more than you think, child. Look how you are careful not to scatter the grain too thickly, and I see how carefully you collect the eggs. You have learned more than you realise, since becoming the mistress of your own establishment. Depend upon it, my dear, Henry has a wife of whom he can be proud, if only you continue to be patient and don't expect the world in a day!'

Although fortified by her mother's kind reassurances, Catherine did not canvass the improbability of a return to Woodston and wondered miserably how she might broach the topic with her father.

Twenty One

The following afternoon, she opened her writing desk and began a new letter to Henry. It gave her much pain to write it, and many a tear was shed over its creamy page, blurring the ink in places, but at last it was written. Wretched, she had just folded the paper and sealed it, when Harriet burst into the room.

'Catherine, Catherine, come quick! Uncle Henry is here! Mama says to tell you. Oh Catherine, may I not go for a ride on his horse, like I did last time he was here? Do say he will let me!'

Catherine was speechless, and in some horror of his coming. 'No, indeed, Harriet, pray don't bother him just now. But what can he mean by coming here?'

Going to the window she was just in time to see Henry dismount his horse, which was puffing and stamping as if it had been ridden at pace. What was the meaning of his coming? Had he not seen the note she had left for him? She hardly knew what to think, but as the sound of his knocking at the door carried upstairs, she knew she could not hide in her room.

Her mother, being unaware of the full extent of the miserable situation in which her daughter found herself, and having a full belief in the goodness of her son-in-law, welcomed Henry into their parlour. But when she observed his very earnest expression and heard his distracted, half-attentive replies to her civil enquires as to his health, she thought it wisest to let the young people at each other, to make up whatever little quarrel they had been labouring under, as soon as possible.

She saw Catherine enter the room, observed the paleness of her cheek, and ushered out the two younger children, leaving Catherin and Henry quite alone.

So little expectation Catherine had had of ever seeing Henry again that she felt herself speechless and quite unequal to this meeting. It took her a few moments to recover her power of speech. 'Do sit, Henry.' She feared her legs would give way. She moved almost dazedly to a seat at the table and took it, without meeting his eyes. Could he really intend to torture her further, to give her more anguish and pain, by his dragging out the unpleasantness, the dreadfulness, of their parting?

Henry had remained standing. He seemed as unhappy as she was. 'Good God, Catherine!' he said after an awkward pause, his hat hanging in his hand. 'I discovered the note you left for me, and I cannot make sense of it. I have no notion of what you intend by your coming away to Fullerton — but tell me at once, is all at an end with us? Do you intend to leave me? You have only to say it and I will disturb you no longer!'

'Why are you come?' replied Catherine in despair, unable to divine his meaning. 'It is not I who has left you — did you not read my note? Can you mean to trample upon my feelings any more thoroughly than you have done? Pray do not torture me any longer!' She stifled a sudden sob into her handkerchief and turned her eyes away.

'I did read your note — and I confess I cannot decipher its meaning! What do you mean by saying you understand what must be done?'

Vexation that Henry would act the innocent with her, of all people, and cause more wretchedness than she already suffered under, made her cheeks pink with mortification. 'How can you pretend with me? I know everything, Henry! I know I have been a foolish, ridiculous wife to you, shaming you in front of your family, and failing at every turn to learn what I ought to have learned from my mother. I am sure I deserve your disgust for it, but do not pretend that you don't love someone else, and wish our marriage at an end! I read the letter from London which you left on your desk!'

Henry now turned white and looked his horror at her words. 'End our marriage? What have you been thinking, what have you been surmising, Catherine? Oh, I am a damned fool indeed!'

'I have only surmised what is clear, from the letter you received from London. You wish to annul our marriage! I left Woodston before you came home to avoid a confrontation. I know I have been a ridiculous wife to you Henry, but you cannot deny that you love Miss Parkhurst and wish our marriage annulled so that you can marry her!'

Henry now seated himself at the table too, and sighed deeply. 'Miss Parkhurst! How do you know about Miss Parkhurst? But never mind that — Catherine, I have been a capital fool. I have wrongly kept many things from you, but let me assure you that my being in love with Miss Parkhurst is not one of them.'

'But — how can you justify — that is, I saw you, that night after the dinner for General Tilney, and you came out of the cellar with her things — you cannot say they are not hers, for I saw the handkerchief myself, clearly, and the initials were "EP." Jenny told me—'

'Jenny! What could *she* know of my feelings! Catherine, I assure you, there was indeed a Miss Parkhurst, but this was long ago. I have been very wrong, but I withheld some information that had come to light recently because I wanted to protect you, but I see I was completely wrong. Can you hear my story, now, although it is too late now to expect you to forgive me?'

Catherine was astonished. 'Forgive you? But no, it is *you* who must forgive *me*! But please, tell me everything, because I am afraid I understand nothing at present!'

Henry, giving her a look of the most speaking kind, began his tale. 'There was a time, Catherine, many years ago now, when I indulged myself in a foolish, youthful infatuation with a young lady. She was but fifteen and I was eighteen. Her father was a friend of my father's, and we developed a hasty but strong attachment. My father forbade a marriage, and so we eloped, to Scotland.'

Catherine was incredulous. 'You were married — in secret!'

'I am not proud of it, Catherine, but it was extremely short-lived, for Eliza's father, discovering her absence and guessing where we had gone, followed us and discovered us only minutes after we had been united. He was excessively angry and took custody of his daughter, but not before we hastily exchanged tokens; I gave her the ring which was upon my finger at the time, and she gave me a lock of her hair and the handkerchief she had about her. Her father removed Eliza directly and vowed that he would have the marriage annulled immediately on the grounds that she was not of age. Defeated in love, I set off, wretchedly miserable, for Northanger.'

'But,' cried Catherine, 'why did you never tell me of it — that you had been married once before?'

Henry had the grace to look abashed. 'I felt myself removed from those events thoroughly, by the long passage of time. After all, Catherine, it was ten years ago, and memories of the lady had faded. Miss Parkhurst had long ceased to be of importance to me, and, as I believed, the marriage had been annulled, and I was never to see her again.'

'What do you mean, you *believed* the marriage had been annulled? It had not?'

Henry sighed. 'I had no reason to believe that Eliza's father had not done as he had said he would, and annulled the marriage immediately. I gave no further thought to enquiring of the outcome of the annulment, for I believed it had taken place. But I learned only recently that it had not. Stay, Catherine, hear me out!'

Catherine had risen, ready to leave the room in shock and distress, but his words stopped her. 'If you were married when we married, then I cannot—'

'Catherine, I was a single man by then — I was a widower. Miss Parkhurst died before you and I had even met. But pray, hear me out to the last, I entreat you!'

'Very well.' She sat again with reluctance and was silent.

Henry continued. 'Colonel Parkhurst, Eliza's father, had suffered a fatal spasm of the heart the very hour he had seized his daughter, and the papers were never drawn up and never taken to the court to be signed. Eliza, consumed from grief, I must suppose, had not thought to make enquiries into the matter; after all, she was but fifteen and I imagine had no idea of legal matters. So we remained, unbeknownst to me, married all that time, although I believed myself free. It was only when Eliza passed last year, before I met you, from a disease of the lungs, that her uncle examined those of her father's papers she had kept in more detail and found among them a letter of advice from the lawyer, dated ten years previously, giving rise to the notion that the annulment had not after all taken place. Further enquiries proved the fact, and a search was made for me, for as Eliza's surviving heir, it seemed that what little she had was, by law, left solely to me.'

'Why, oh why, did you not tell me!' Catherine did not know if she was angry or relieved. How could Henry had hidden such things from her?

'Do you remember that day when I received a letter which put me in a very bad state of mind – before I went to London on business? I was a bearish husband to you then, I'm afraid, and I'm heartily sorry for it. But that letter was from Eliza's uncle, informing me of all that had passed, and that I was Eliza Parkhurst's beneficiary. What little she had had to leave was now mine, it seemed. I posted straight to London, and sought advice from my attorney there. He arranged to have the marriage annulled in retrospect, as I wished all her belongings to go to her family. It took some time, Catherine, and I'm afraid I was so angry at myself for having deceived you that I felt unable to bear it, to see your face, to remember your trust in me, when I had let you down so thoroughly. I became distant and cold, I know, for I was weighed down with guilt.'

'And you stayed away for longer and longer hours, keeping your distance from me. It pained me so very much, Henry, to think I might have lost your love! I blamed myself, for having made such a dreadful job of running a household!'

'I can never forgive myself, Catherine, and I can hope only to allay your misery by assuring you it was all my own fault, and none of yours!'

'What happened after that?' asked Catherine, hope brewing in her breast.

'I waited to hear news of the annulment's having taken place. It was not as if I needed it, for I was legally her widowed husband, but considering I had thought myself free all those years, I did not feel that it was right in the eyes of God and man to allow such a thing to go unaltered by law, if I could hope to make things right. I gave instructions for a solicitor to take the case before magistrate's court, and to hear the case. That letter you saw on my desk a few days ago was the news I had been waiting for, that the request for the annulment had been accepted and all that was left for me to do was to sign the papers and I would no longer be Eliza Parkhurst's windowed husband. It made right the wrong that had been done these many years ago. My dear girl, can you accept my explanation and give me a chance to prove my love for you?'

Catherine had begun to feel a growing hope on hearing Henry's term of endearment, but still, she had to put to bed the worst of her fears. 'But did you love her — do you still love her?' asked Catherine, in dread of the reply.

'My dearest Kitty, let me assure you that I long ceased to think of Miss Parkhurst shortly after the affair. I realized very quickly that it had been nothing but boyish infatuation, foolish calf love, and I quickly came to realise my fortunate escape from such a marriage. Many have thus married and lived to repent such a union based only on physical attraction. I do not doubt of my own unhappiness if the marriage had continued. I am sorry for poor Eliza,' he added sadly, 'who never married, and left this world in a wretched circumstance, but believe in your heart, my dear, that I have long ceased to feel anything for her.'

'There is one thing I cannot account for however,' replied a troubled Catherine. 'Why did you keep the tokens she gave you in the cellar here? And why did you later remove them — the night of the dinner party?"

'One day, I came across them in the bottom of a drawer where I had laid them many years ago. When I found them, I had since met *you*, Catherine, and you had stolen my heart. To have destroyed them perhaps would have been a wiser thing, but I felt it was wrong, and that some day they might be returned to the lady, or given away. So I put them deep in the cellar, where they would be away from us and our life. I had forgotten them but when the letter came from the solicitor, I removed them, for I intended to give them over to the solicitor, to surrender them to her family. They will mean more to her family than they could to me.'

'And your mother's things? Why did you not make a present of them to me after they were found? I know I have disappointed you, but it was one more thing which spoke to me of your increasing indifference to me.'

'I sent them away to be cleaned, Catherine, that is all. I wish you to have them, but they were tainted by Frederick's misuse of them, and I felt that to have them cleaned and set in a pretty box, you might look more favourably upon my gift. You shall have them very soon, as soon as you wish it.'

Catherine absorbed all that Henry had told her, and observing his keen looks, she ventured, 'And you are not angry with me, and wish me gone? I cannot blame you, for I have been such a trial to you! I have ruined your cravats, and lost one of the hens, and I cannot even play the piano-forte well enough for you to sing even though I did intend to practice every day, only I dislike it so much, and you have such a wonderful voice, Henry, and I am so very—'

'—and you are so very wonderful, and you have worked so very hard, and I am not the least bit disgusted or angry at you, you silly, beautiful pea-goose!'

Henry smiled at her with such devotion that she needed no other proof of his feelings. 'So you really did not intend to annul our marriage — I thought — oh Henry!' So overcome with relief that she was, she could hardly believe it was true. 'I thought you were disgusted with me and my foolish efforts to become accomplished and to impress you and your family. I have been so mistaken, so wrong-minded, that I can hardly think of it without blushing. I have embarrassed you, and made a mockery of Woodston! I ought never to have ventured into that cellar at all, and none of this would have happened, for I would have been none the wiser! I have failed you and I am heartily ashamed of myself! It is no wonder that I thought you wished our marriage dissolved! Can you ever forgive me?'

'Foolish girl indeed!' Henry now came forward took up her hands in his own and spoke with feeling. 'You could never disappoint me, Kitty; it is I who must beg *your* forgiveness. I have not only been dishonest, when I ought to have been frank and open, but I have let you down badly. If you had not gone into the cellar, if your curiosity had not led you there, you would not have discovered Frederick's betrayal, and my own, neither! I am a base fool, and it *was* betrayal, when I look at it squarely between the eyes! I have neglected you and allowed worldly concerns to overtake my good sense, and worse, to prevent me being a good husband to you. I *did* neglect you. My conduct these last weeks past has been reprehensible in every respect. It mortifies me deeply when I reflect how much you have tried, how giving you have been, and how much you have sacrificed for my sake. I have tried your patience with evils of the most detestable kind. Little wonder you wish to run far from Woodston and return to Fullerton. And yet, I beg you, will you come home, my dear, dear Kitty? Will you come home to Woodston?'

At these words, Catherine was much affected, and was about to answer in the affirmative, but then recalled something that caused her to pale. 'There is something I must confess, Henry, and I pray that you will not be vexed with me.'

'There is nothing that could make me vexed with you, my dear.'

'Then I must tell you before I lose my nerve — Mr Longstaff come upon me in the garden three days ago, while I was in a great anxiety, and I told him about the letter I had found, and my fears that you were still in love with this Miss Parkhurst. I — I am afraid, that he tried to — to take a liberty with me, and I dismissed him.'

Henry uttered a short, angry exclamation, and Catherine rushed to add, 'Pray do not be angry with me, but I was so vexed that I could not bear him to torture me when I was in so much anguish at the thought of losing you. I cannot bear to have him around me, and I am most sorry if I gave him any idea of my allowing any such liberties, but if I did give him to imagine that anything he might say or do would be acceptable to me, I was not sensible of it.'

'Angry with you, Catherine? No, indeed, I am not angry with you, but I am incredulous that he tried to impose upon you — and yet, you have been so courageous as to dismiss him! Catherine, do you not realise how much you have learned and how far you have come? You have acted according to your very admirable character — you have dismissed Mr Longstaff, which took great courage, I collect, and Mrs Poulter too — yes, I know she has gone away, and that you dismissed her, although no one was able to say why — but it does not signify, except that you were bold enough to do it! You approached Frederick and forced him to confess his actions to my father. That took great courage also. You put me to shame, my dear. I thought,' he added humbly, 'that in our union, I might add something to your life, to improve *your* character, and now I see I was entirely mislead in the matter — it is you who have taught *me*, and set an example for what *my* behaviour must be.'

'Oh Henry!' was all that Catherine could utter, and then she was weeping, and Henry's arms were around her, and he was tenderly kissing away her tears and uttering the most tender apologies. Catherine in her turn was filled with relief, and the heavy weight which she had carried around for many weeks finally relieved itself, and in its place she was filled with happiness.

After some time in which neither of them spoke, Catherine heard some giggling from beyond the door. Striding to the door, she swung it open. Harriet and George collapsed upon the floor, giggling. 'We saw you kissing Henry through the keyhole!' announced a pink-faced Harriet.

Catherine exchanged glances with Henry and laughed. 'Go and find Mama and tell her I am going home with Henry. Now!' she ordered, unable to suppress her amusement.

As her little brother and sister ran upstairs, Catherine turned to Henry. 'I want to go home to Woodston, if you will have me,' she said quietly. 'I know I have been foolish girl, but I will try to grow every day into a wife of whom you can be proud.'

'I am already proud of you, Kitty. I only hope I can become the husband you deserve.' He kissed her again most tenderly. 'And I hope that you know that my attachment to you can cease only with my life.'

'Oh Henry!' Catherine returned his kisses, then pulled away a little. 'There is another reason I wish to return to Woodston,' she told him, suddenly shy.

Henry looked his enquiry.

'I wish to new-furnish the little sitting-room beside our bedroom.'

Henry looked puzzled. 'Whatever for? My father just recently had it papered, and the furniture is not yet more than a few years old — but if you wish it —' Here he stopped short, for Catherine had taken his hand and placed it on her gown, below her waistline. Henry was puzzled for moment, then a slow smile overspread his countenance. He gave her a most speaking look, and she smiled back.

'Are you certain?' he asked.

'I think so. We are going to have a child, Henry.'

Henry looked down upon his wife's blooming face, saw with pleasure the pink which flushed her cheeks.

'I collect,' he remarked with a glint in his eye, 'that we might just have the happy ever after you expected four months ago, after all!'

'Yes,' replied his wife, taking his hand in her own, 'but before we do that, I rather think you had better let Harriet ride on your horse again or we will never hear the end of it!'

Twenty Two

I suppose that the reader will now expect, nay, demand, to hear that Henry and Catherine lived for ever after a life of perfect felicity and contentment, and that nothing ever came again to mar their happiness. I shall not promise this, for *that* promise, I hold, is a rash one, and cannot bode well simply on the grounds that any such promise might well tempt providence once again. But I shall tell you that Henry and Catherine finally found a pretty steady nuptial bliss, or as near to it as any two generally rational and sensible young people who are just starting out in married life might come. It augers well that Catherine and Henry are both blessed with more than the common degree of good sense and sufficiency of character, to make them perfectly able to navigate the usual rough spots which marriage inevitably brings. Certainly, in Henry and Catherine's case, the adversity of yesterday most likely will work to make them stronger, and wiser, tomorrow.

As for the marriage of Captain Frederick Tilney to Miss Thorpe, who can say the two people may not promote and improve the happiness of the other? Miss Thorpe has, after all, got the man she wanted, and Captain Tilney a fortune to spend. When two parties are united by similar characters, whether those characters be moral or immoral, and deceitful and cunning altogether, who can know what the power of a common cause cannot achieve. I can, however, state with great authority that Captain and Mrs Isabella Tilney were never invited to Woodston, for Henry, despite being thought in general to have an accommodating character, would not countenance the possibility of giving his wife the vexation and anxiety that such a visit from the new occupants of Northanger would surely afford.

And finally, I must leave it to be settled by whomsoever may read it, whether the tendency of this work be altogether to discourage husbandly neglect, or to reward wifely curiosity.

The End

I hope that you've enjoyed this book!

After the About the Author section, you'll find a preview of

The Value of an Anne Elliot

About the Author

Kate Westwood is the author's pseudonym. Kate has a background in academic writing and holds a Master's degree in English Literature. Having had a life-long dream to write, she finally turned her pen to regency romance when she turned fifty.

Kate is a huge fan of Austen, and her contemporaries, and strives to recreate an authentic 'regency' experience for the reader.

Kate's hobbies, when she is not writing or reading Regency romance, include playing classical piano, and walking and hiking the beautiful Gold Coast Hinterland. Kate has three adult sons and lives in the beautiful Moreton Bay Islands with her partner and cat.

Connect with Kate

Facebook: https://www.facebook.com/katewestwood.net/
Sign up to Kate's email newsletter at :
www.katewestwood.net
to receive the subscriber exclusive story *'The Gift'* as a welcome gift!

Here is your preview of
The Value of an Anne Elliot

Prologue

Friday, 26 May, 1815
London, White's Club.

The letter smelled faintly of almonds. What others might have described as a cloying, sickly scent, brought to him the steadying reminder of all that he owed. Family was everything.

He ran his thumb along the edge of the paper. He could not fault the folding of it. It was perfectly executed. As always. On the front, the direction was written in black ink; the sure but delicate hand did the perfect folds no disservice. Turning the letter over, he perceived the shape of a rose imprinted into the black sealing wax. He smiled, understanding immediately. He enjoyed a private quiz, and his sister's singular humour never disappointed him. Oh, how true the old saying that it takes one to know one.

He had understood his older sister from a young age. She was like a cipher, a hieroglyphic, that only he knew how to read. Her spoken word and her meaning were always two different things, and his survival instincts, always strong, had taught him at an early age to learn her particular language. He had learned from her too, that there were always two ways to read things; the way they were presented on the surface, and the hidden meanings that lay below, he thought, eyeing the black rose. There is always, he pondered, something to be found below the surface if one is prepared to hunt for it. A shrewd practiser of the art of obfuscation in his own dealings, he appreciated the same approach in the one person to whom he was closest in life. He had assuredly learned from his sister the art of concealment. Perhaps their characters were too similar, because they almost never quarrelled. Was that a fault? Mim would say that it was. But he could not imagine anyone else with whom he could be of so similar a mind, and in so perfect a harmony.

She came and went at her own volition, following her own will, and he suffered under no misapprehensions; her will was iron clothed in velvet. But he would always be ready to escort her, with the greatest degree of solicitous attention, anywhere she desired to go, in his own carriage, at his own expense, and at a moment's notice. He would do whatever she bade him, no questions asked. He could do no less for the older sister who had fought for him when he needed a protector, mothered him when he was young and motherless. Even now, she always took his part with the fierce loyalty with which two siblings, united by blood then orphaned together and left almost to raise themselves, would most naturally find themselves bound. He had on several occasions got himself into one or other kind of difficulty, and she had always beat him an easy path from trouble's door.

Therefore, if she summoned, he came, and was glad to obey. The symbol of the rose and the scent of bitter almond was her own gentle reminder of the lengths she would go to, if needed, for his sake. He neither needed, nor minded, this conjuring of his memory. He was every day grateful. Family was everything. The *only* thing.

He lifted his eyes. The salon was empty and the air cool at that time of morning. The numerous brown leather chairs which were arranged in comfortable twos and threes around small tables of chestnut and rosewood were vacant, most fellows not having risen yet. Almost nobody ever showed his head through the front door of White's before midday, and even one o'clock in the afternoon was early for those who went to bed at five in the morning after a night of drinking and gaming. For himself, he took great pleasure in being thought singular and made a point of rising early, even when he had been up all night, much to the ire of his sleep-deprived valet.

He enjoyed being at his club. Since his election several years ago he had taken a quiet pleasure in the air of respectful reserve which each member preserved so studiously, while still managing to engage in the usual pastimes found in such halls, in that jovial and 'hail-fellow-well-met' fashion which was the glue which held them together in brotherhood. Along with his other vices, he unashamedly considered himself an inveterate gambler, and it suited both his taste for the tables, and his reticence with regard to his private life, to have a membership at White's. Here he found a gentle camaraderie, mingled with that terribly English tendency to insularity which resulted in never having one's privacy intruded upon. It allowed him an easy existence; welcomed by his fellows, he would pick up the threads of a conversation here and there, and toss off a few of the usual earthy remarks expected in a roomful of males, but he could exclude company just as easily, and without question, if he wished it. And best of all, he never had to talk about his past. Or his present, for that matter. They all accepted him for what he appeared to be, and if anything, they merely smiled at the tales which sometimes followed him through the front door. It was *Town*, after all.

Now, in the early morning sun was only just brushing the furniture with pale gold through the heavy damask window drapery, and he revelled in the quiet of the room. Those morning street noises, the clatter of carts and bustle of self-important servants moving about with baskets of cabbages and fish, the strident calling out of various purveyors, none of these assaults could be heard from the behind the white stone walls separating those within them from the dirty streets. The fetid summer stench of the road, which arose from the mingling of human urine and horse droppings, was also barred from the club by the means of two front doors, and the boot room in between. It was not that he despised the street, but when he entered into the quiet, elegant world behind those stone walls, he expected the street to wait outside, until he was ready, like a servant awaiting his orders.

Leaning forward, he now took up from the table the ornate letter knife which lay there and applied it under the wax seal of the paper. Separating the black wax from the paper, he was careful to leave the rose emblem unbroken, and he opened the letter out.

The heavy, heady scent of almond filled his nostrils. He stretched out in the chair and drew his breath in forcefully, enjoying the rush of pleasure in his temples, and that odd but welcome feeling the scent of her letters always gave him, as if his sister was in the same room with him. The scent of her was like opium vapour, he thought, but without the stupor afterwards, better than the best Macouba snuff.

He read over the letter:

> *Bennett-Street, Bath.*
> *Wednesday 24 May*

> *'Haro darling,*

> *Well, here I have been for six weeks, and I cannot tell you how tedious it is getting with me and dear Leticia. You know I love my own sister quite as much as I ought but I confess that I am becoming disenchanted with Bath. The place is ill-designed for prolonged stays, with the weather so dreary and the people so bland. It wearies me, so long we have been here, and all the amusements that we ran mad for in the first weeks have palled. I long for your company again! You are always the only person who can relieve my tedium! And you surely must have had your fun in London by now, if I have it right, for I always give you six to eight weeks until boredom sets in. Am I not a canny mathematician? Are you weary of her yet? I know she is young and innocent and sweet but even you must tire of that cloying, sweet innocence sometime! And besides that, you naughty boy, you know it will not be long before the papa finds you out! Pray do not get into another fight, Haro. You cannot expect me to get you out of yet another scrape! Be a good fellow and leave London and come to me in Bath.*

> *There is another reason I ask you to come to Bath. Do you remember what we discussed at the*

Parsonage before we parted? Well, I have a scheme to put to you, and even you must approve it! My new acquaintance here, with whom I am on the most intimate terms, is the eldest daughter of a crusty old baronet who has made his home here in Bath, a Sir Walter Elliot. I made their acquaintance almost immediately on my arrival six weeks ago, almost quite as soon as I singled the lady out as a prospect for you.

Elizabeth Elliot is a woman of refined air, good breeding, and is quite marriageable despite her thirty odd years. I can vouchsafe to say, that while I perceive a certain strength of character and a tolerable superiority of mind, she is nothing compared to the strength of two people together, united by blood and a shared past. No indeed, the poor creature, while possessing enough common wit, rank, and superior beauty to make her acceptable in any drawing room in Mayfair, will not, I collect, give us any trouble. She is too distracted with increasing her own consequence to understand others on anything but a superficial level. She is, in short, perfect to our purpose.

Now, since you have solemnly promised me that you will settle down and make me some nephews and nieces to amuse us when we are at E, I have done my part and secured her trust. I have painted her a darling picture of you, and now you must come and play your part in attaching her early affections. She has recently been low in spirits; a young man, who has gone away and married someone else, or some such thing — you know how it is — her hopes on that score were sadly dashed, and you, Haro, can arrive just at the right time to soothe her feelings and pamper the flame of her self-importance until she is charmed and under your spell! I really do think you could have her with a very little effort, and she is quite a beauty, for all her one-and-thirty years.

Yes, I really do think you will approve. There is no tedious piety or false modesty with this one – one Miss FP is enough, I collect, for us both! – do you recall how enamoured of her you once were? – nor is she of a sulking bent as with your spoilt Mrs R; no, this one is quite full of the right airs and manners which a good birth bestows, and she will be tolerably endowed upon her father's demise. And that cannot be far off, for I have never seen so choleric an appearance in a person since our aunt's illness.

I believe, Haro, that an alliance with Miss Elliot would be a match to befit your status, your fortune, and your breeding. Matrimony, my dear boy, is your duty, and you cannot ignore duty forever or it will catch you and have its way. Better to choose than be chosen! And you know we must both do what we must. I, too, must do my duty in turn. We must stem the tide of gossip and besides that, you know that we must preserve E by means of an heir.

Come soon. You must take a house in a good part of town. It will not suit our purpose to be too modest if we are to catch us an Elliot. I shall arrange to engage a house in Laura-place or Williams-street for you directly. Darling boy, I believe you must congratulate me on my genius! Come early next week and we shall have a pleasant coze on it all,

Your loving
Mim.

P.S. Were you not diverted to see the wax seal? I shall adopt it always now. It amuses me excessively!

He put down the letter carefully on the varnished side table near his hand. So, his sister had made good on her word and found him a female, modestly rich, with breeding and airs and pride. He played idly with the condensation on his glass, the expensive ice within shifting inside its little bath of excellent whiskey. If he *must* marry, he thought, that is precisely the kind of woman he should like; a proud, haughty woman would suit his nature well, for he could take pleasure in taming her and making her fall in love with him. He had powers of pleasing enough to put a hole in the heart of any woman he chose. Even cold little Fanny Price had not been immune — he had *almost* managed to cage her up like a little bird, a little bird he would have found much pleasure in amusing himself with — but he stopped himself and gave a short, mirthless laugh. *She* was not worth his time. How glad he was that she had backed out of the engagement! Yes, this one sounded more to his taste. But thirty years old! Ah well, but he could not expect to have all his tastes catered to. Besides, these silly little sweet, young things that it seemed was all London afforded these days, tired him easily. The little innocent he had been dallying with here in town was already becoming a bore to him, but he hadn't quite finished with her yet.

Reaching into his pocket with his left hand, he withdrew a small, ivory carved box and opened its painted lid. Pinching a small amount of fragrant snuff within in his fingers, he placed it on the back of his right hand and bent his nostrils to the powder, sharply inhaling twice. His eyes watered and he delicately wiped away the tears, then the residue, from his nose and hands with a cloth he always kept for the purpose.

He leaned back contentedly in his chair. Three more days and he would do his sister's bidding and get himself to Bath to play the marriage game, but he had some pleasures of the flesh to extract first.

One

Thursday 1 June, 1815
Kellynch Hall, Somersetshire.

'A letter, my dear, just now arrived.'

The gentle, enquiring voice which interrupted his reverie was an intrusion into the quiet morning light of the library, but not an unwelcome one. Putting down his pen and blotting the ink of his correspondence, Captain Frederick Wentworth smiled with tender regard at the open, pretty face of the woman before him. He took the letter from her hand. 'I shall have done in a few minutes. Tell Sophie I will come to breakfast shortly.'

He had been expecting orders any day, although he had hoped fervently that they might be as delayed as would not injure the greater good, so that he might remain at Kellynch as long as possible. But both he and Anne knew what the letter contained, and the risk attending his career had been known to them both before they had married.

His wife stood a moment more, hesitating, her pale blue muslin morning dress providing a pleasant foil to the pink-blushed cheeks and dark hair above. He fancied privately that his Anne was lately so altered in plumpness and in good looks that he could hardly think her recognisable from the creature he had met with last year at Uppercross. 'Go to breakfast, my dear. I will come directly.'

He watched his wife retreat, pondering as he did so often these days, his good fortune. With Anne he had found an unexpected happiness that he had never brooked upon. She was always so right, so capable, so dependable! She seemed so in harmony with his own thoughts and so sensible of his wishes, that he marvelled not for the first time that he had gained such a creature!

Very lately married, he had come to value ever more the quiet, gentle soul which was the Anne Elliot he loved! Three months of marriage had taught him nothing he did not already know, except the increasing strength of his passion for the woman who had taught *him* in turn, of the value of abiding constancy in love. All the success he had ever enjoyed as captain of the Asp and then of the Laconia, all the material manifestations of his achievements, he now realised as falsely valued, when compared with the gaining of a treasure such as an Anne Elliot!

Smiling slightly still, he returned to appraise gravely the handwriting on the letter, feeling that he apprehended already the contents of the sealed paper. A minute's reading and his suspicions were confirmed. Rear Admiral Malcom had arrived in the country the previous day and had posted immediately to London to report. Two months previously the Great Powers had declared Napoleon an outlaw and had vowed to destroy his power in Europe. Another war was now inevitable. Each power had deployed one hundred and fifty thousand men on the ground, and Wentworth was certain that there would now be a request for naval reinforcements in Europe. The letter was lowered, and some moment spent in serious reflection, his face thoughtful.

His countenance had never suffered the rigours that other sailors suffered, even while his father-in-law liked to declare, out of his hearing, that his son-in-law was well-looking enough but had not escaped a sailor's ill fortune of always seeming slightly weather-beaten. However, it was a fact acknowledged by most of his acquaintance, that Captain Frederick Wentworth not only had never lost his good looks, but that they had seemed only to improve with the advance of years, despite their being subject to several seasons at sea and enough battles to bring him home a handsome fortune.

Now, happy in love and comfortable in marriage, he might have been said to glow with vitality, even if that glow was at present overhung with anxiety for the news he was about to impart. He knew Anne would be waiting for him in the morning room, at breakfast with his sister and Admiral Croft, and it was there he made for with reluctant haste.

He leaned his head into the doorway of the morning parlour and took in the charming domestic scene. His sister, Mrs Croft, still sat at breakfast, and Admiral Croft, her husband, had taken up the paper and made himself comfortable. Her own breakfast finished, Anne sat with her husband's socks, darning tools at her side. This task she always insisted was her own, for it gave her, she said, a way to render what small service she could for the husband who had made her happy beyond whatever she could have hoped for only six months ago! With Anne, her pleasure was to always give way, her joy was to serve. He marvelled, smiled to himself, and entered the parlour. Anne immediately put down the stockings she had taken up and raised enquiring brows.

It was, however, Mrs Croft who spoke first. 'Frederick! Have you come for some tea? Janet, make a fresh pot, if you please. Now do sit, Frederick. You find us lately risen, for poor Matthew has the gout again and we have been discussing the possibility of Bath, for the waters; it did him such good in February, and Anne agrees, but now that Anne is —'

'Ah!' interjected Wentworth hastily, 'that is not good news, I fear! I am sorry to hear of your trouble, Admiral, but I have sobering news myself, I am afraid.'

He proffered the letter first to his wife, who took it and perused it with great seriousness in her large, dark eyes.

Mrs Croft sighed with the resignation only a seasoned sailor's wife could summon, and said, 'I take it you have had news? Has the War Office written to you? Shall they send forces to Ghent after all?' and at the same time, Admiral Croft ventured, 'Ah, so it has come to this, then, aye but it was naught that was not expected. Perhaps you shan't be away long, Frederick?'

Wentworth, however, only had eyes for his wife, who, after looking over the letter, was as composed as she was serious.

She put aside the letter and began calmly, 'It was what we have all been in expectation of, and of course, I shall be well looked after here. I cannot hope for more, and you must follow your duty.

But what do you comprehend from this news? Surely you will get orders very soon. Do you expect to be called away today?' Her voice was steady, and her countenance tolerably composed, even though she was to lose her husband only two months after their marriage, to his other wife, the ship which he would command his attention for perhaps several months, or even more!

He admired her composure, and taking her hand, smiled into her dark brown eyes. He could not but help glance at her smooth muslin dress, and the pleasing new plumpness it concealed. 'You are too good, too forbearing,' he replied in a low voice meant only for Anne, 'but it is more concerning to me that I must leave you alone, perhaps for many weeks—'

But before Anne could remonstrate, the admiral, slightly deaf in both ears, had already seized the letter and perused its contents. 'So, Frederick,' he interposed comfortably, so that Wentworth paused mid-speech to Anne. 'What do you make of the news?' The admiral was quite composed, so much acquainted with years of practice in the first alarms of war and letters of summons that he could not but remain unmoved at the idea of another battle. 'I judge that Malcolm's new appointment to Rear Admiral by Wellington was a wise one, and if he is posted up to London so soon after his return, I am persuaded they will give him plenty to do. He is a capital kind of man, quite well enough acquainted with the rigours of working with the army to assist with supporting the Allies. I wonder though, what is the Duke's aim; I suppose they might send the navy to Martinique or perhaps to Europe, although what good can be done by a presence there I cannot tell.'

'Pardon me, Admiral, but I believe the scheme of offering assistance will require Wellington's presence in Ghent or Brussels; on that score, I collect you may be right, Sophie.' He glanced at his sister. 'Bonaparte's advance toward Belgium must be considered a decided threat to that city.'

Anne turned to her husband. 'And we have expected this summons ever since Bonaparte's escape from Elba; I am not overcome by surprise, Frederick. We two will be well looked after, whatever this may mean for the next few months.' She ran a hand self-consciously over her dress, smoothing the fabric over her belly. To his eye, there was the merest hint of a roundedness that he had not seen before, but to others it must be yet invisible.

Wentworth gave his wife the singular glance that only a besotted husband, newly to be a father, can give. 'You must promise me to take care of yourself, and our child. I wish fervently that I did not have to go away—'

Mrs Croft stopped him mid-sentence. 'I despise to hear you talk of Anne as if she were a delicate creature, Frederick, unable to stand an absence of a few months,' she scolded him affectionately. 'Of course, it is always the way with us navy wives, is it not Anne, that there will be a *little* anxiety, but we are made of sturdier stuff than what could only suffer calm waters; I shall be here, and Uppercross not so far distant, and I vouch that the time will pass quickly enough until we welcome you back, brother! Meanwhile, let us not alarm Anne unduly, especially in her delicate condition, for it is but a trifle of news that need not alarm anyone to a great degree until we have just cause to feel it!'

'Sophie, you are quite right,' said her brother placatingly, 'and I still have no definite orders, nor a set departure date, although I apprehend it cannot be long, with this summoning of Malcom. They mean to support the action in some way, and it cannot be more than a day or so before I am called away, I think!'

'Let us hope that the action, whatever form it takes, will be swift and sure then,' added the admiral. 'My dear,' he said, turning to his wife, 'It would be best to delay this scheme of going up to Bath, until we hear where Frederick is to be stationed, don't you agree?'

'Oh,' cried Anne in quick embarrassment to give such trouble, 'pray don't let my husband's impending orders prevent you from taking the waters at Bath, Admiral; you know how they do you good! I could go to Mary, or really, I am quite well enough to remain at Kellynch, until your return!'

'Nonsense, Anne,' cried Mrs Croft kindly, 'we wouldn't hear of going away to leave you alone, and besides, it will only be small delay, until things are settled, and then you might come with us, perhaps! Or we might all go into Shropshire, since my brother Edward has been quite forceful in his entreaties to visit him and Catherine and the new baby. Anne must come with us — I do favour Bath for the admiral's gout — but wherever we are, Frederick, Anne will always have a home, be assured of that!'

His sister was all amiable condescension, all sisterly affection. Wentworth received her assurances gratefully and told her so. 'It is too bad though, to be called away at such a time—' he said, thinking of Anne's impending confinement.

Mrs Croft would not be put off. 'Pray don't think on it, Frederick, we look upon Anne quite as our own family, you know; it would be unthinkable to leave her behind here. No, she shall go to Bath when and if we are satisfied that you are stationed safely wherever you shall be sent.'

Wentworth joined with Anne in giving them his thanks again, and not for the first time had reason to be grateful his sister and the Admiral had offered them a home until the threat of war had passed and he and Anne could purchase a cosy establishment of their own. Now, more than ever, it occurred to him the good in the scheme, for Anne would be close to Uppercross and could have the daily care and attention of her own sister during her confinement. He was both excited by the thought of being a father, and naturally anxious, and his sister's being present to support Anne would be a vast relief to his mind as he went to war once again.

'It quite escaped my mind, but I have had a letter from Mary this morning,' said Anne, breaking into her husband's thoughts. 'Poor Henrietta has come over with a bad cold; it is very bad luck so soon after the wedding, poor girl, and Mary is convinced she will catch it,' she added, suppressing a smile. 'Perhaps I might invite Mary and the children to come here for a few days, if you will say yes, Mrs Croft,' she added, 'It might do Mary good to have a change of environment. All the excitement of change has belonged to everyone else these last weeks, and I think my sister feels as if she has been left out a little.'

Mrs Croft was gracious. 'Why of course, Anne! This is just as much your home as it is ours, and you must know you can never stand on ceremony with us, can she Matthew, or we would be quite offended! You must ask your sister and the children to come away here, before we make for Bath, if we go at all, of course.'

Wentworth said with amusement, 'I collect that your sister has had all the excitement of the Musgrove sisters' double wedding, and a large breakfast, to give her some not so *very* insignificant object to attend lately.'

'Yes, my dear,' replied Anne, 'but you know how Mary disapproves both the matches; I think she still feels it keenly that Henrietta married a country curate instead of a captain.' Her eyes danced.

'Aye, it would be wonderful indeed, if every woman was as fortunate,' he laughed.

'And Louisa Benwick is in Lyme with her husband and the Harvilles, I believe?' reminded Mrs Croft. 'Then your sister must want for company. I collect it will be dull enough at Uppercross for her to welcome a little change of scenery.'

Admiral Croft inclined his head and added his own earnest entreaties to invite them at once, and Wentworth, who was applied to by his sister, agreed it was a good scheme, for it would distract Anne from the thought that he was to go away soon.

'Then I shall write my reply,' answered Anne, 'and invite them as soon as they can come.'

Later, when they retired to bed, Anne sat up against the pillows with her husband. 'I shall enjoy a visit from Mary and the children. Your sister is so very kind, but I confess I shall miss you terribly when you are called away. The children, I am sure, will be a great distraction.'

Wentworth, knowing Mary Musgrove to sometimes be missing those little touches of sensitive kindness toward her older sibling said, 'Don't forget that Sophie is as much your sister now as she is mine! And Edward a brother! You shall meet him in due course. I hope Mary treats you with more than the usual amount of civility and kindness now that you will both have something more in common than only a mother and father!'

'I am afraid, as much as I dearly love my sister, she will take as little pleasure in my condition as she has done in her own! To Mary, bearing children is an inconvenience! But even if my sister is neglectful, I shall barely regard it, for I will have the dear children, and in them I shall have real affection and an object of interest and amusement. Yes, they shall do me good, I collect!'

Wentworth took her hand earnestly. 'I expect orders tomorrow or in the next week at most, but I can only hope, with all my heart, to be home in time to greet our child into the world!'

Anne only squeezed his hand gently, would not weep although she longed to, and leaned over to blow out the candle.

Read the rest of

The Value of an Anne Elliot

Get it at
https://www.amazon.com/dp/B08Q7SMLQD/

Go to
www.katewestwood.net
and sign up to Kate's newsletter for release notices and more!

Other Books by Kate Westwood

A Scandal at Delford
Beauty and the Beast of Thornleigh
A Bath Affair
The Value of an Anne Elliot